TRACES

BLOOD BROTHER

MALCOLM ROSE

Author's Note:
With special thanks to The Workhouse
who allowed the copyright lyrics of 'Look up at the Stars'
to masquerade in these pages as the work of Jade Vernon
(p.163) and in the imagination of Luke Harding (p.215)

All of the experiments described in these pages
as the work of the fictional Institute of Biomechanical Research
have been carried out in actual laboratories

First published 2008 by Kingfisher
an imprint of Macmillan Children's Books
a division of Macmillan Publishers Limited
20 New Wharf Road, London N1 9RR
Basingstoke and Oxford
Associated companies throughout the world
www.panmacmillan.com

ISBN: 978-0-7534-1541-2

Text copyright © Malcolm Rose 2008

The right of Malcolm Rose to be identified as the
author of this work has been asserted by him in accordance
with the Copyright, Designs and Patents Act 1988.

1 3 5 7 9 8 6 4 2

A CIP catalogue record for this book is available from the British Library.

Printed in India
1TR/1107/THOM/(THOM)/80STORA/C

Visit **www.panmacmillan.com** to read more about all our books
and to buy them. You will also find features, author interviews and
news of any author events, and you can sign up for e-newsletters
so that you're always first to hear about our new releases.

TRACES

BLOOD BROTHER

MALCOLM ROSE

KINGFISHER

ABOUT THE AUTHOR

Malcolm Rose, a former Senior Lecturer in Chemistry, is a well-known children's thriller writer of some 32 novels including six *Traces* titles. Malcolm has won the Angus Book Award and the Lancashire Book of the Year Award. His books regularly feature in the Book Trust 100 best books for children list and *Traces: Final Lap* was selected for the *Riveting Reads: Boys into Books* list. In the USA, *Traces: Framed!* was selected as a Best International Book by the International Reading Association. Malcolm lives in Sheffield.

Chapter One

Nyree was nervous and scared, but she was also spellbound. With her personal tutor, she'd come to a halt beside a rock garden of colourful heathers that surrounded a scruffy wooden hut in the picturesque riverside quarter of York. "Well," she said with a tremor in her voice, "this must be it." Nyree's sunken eyes were fixed on the shack that had once been very showy. Its bright paintwork was now faded and peeling, revealing rotten wood underneath. Even though the cabin had seen better days, its windows had displays of cheerful homemade trinkets. They were the reason Nyree Max had sought out the trailer before going back into hospital.

When Mr Peacock opened the door cautiously, a distinct smell of herbs and spices wafted over Nyree. Scented candles lit the place and an old man was sitting behind a counter, tying together sprigs of a deep green and crimson heather. Nyree took one look at him and knew at once that he was the artist with the peculiar reputation. She mounted the two steps and entered the hut uneasily. At least in the shack the blinding winter sunshine would no longer burn her eyes and blur her vision.

The old man raised his face towards his visitors. He

cast a dismissive glance at Mr Peacock but he gazed intently at Nyree. His expression suggested a mixture of kindliness and pity. He did not utter a word.

The door closed behind Mr Peacock, shutting Nyree and her instructor inside. The flimsy cabin was curiously quiet, cut off from the rest of York. Around three of its walls were shelves and in the middle was a long table. All of the available surfaces were covered with the artist's goods: cute cats and dogs carved delicately in wood, countless model dancers in pink or blue with silver head-dresses, dainty porcelain figurines, candles infused with herbs, ceramic boxes and much more. Carefully, Nyree picked up a few of the mementoes, one after the other, but felt no attachment to them. She replaced them at once.

Making her way down the aisle between the table and the right-hand shelving, Nyree hesitated by a selection of jade ornaments and jewellery. Handwritten on a little card among the trinkets were the words: "Items in hard jade bring the owner good health". Reading the label, Nyree allowed herself a sad smile. Hoping it was true, she picked up a jade squirrel, weighed it in her hand and then put it back on the display. There were many clever carvings in jade: coiled snakes, pigs, grotesque little men, all sorts. None of them grabbed her attention.

Then, a lush green pyramid caught Nyree's eye. It was solid and simple. This was no fancy carving, just three slick surfaces in dark green. She put out her trembling hand towards it but did not clasp the ornament. For a moment, she felt frightened of it. She told herself not to be silly. She tried to convince herself that her unease was nothing to do with the pyramid. She was just afraid of letting the stylish charm slip from her fingers and crash to the floor. She was weak of course, but not that weak. Her eyesight was wobbly, but not that wobbly. The tingling in her spine and the thudding inside her head were her illness. Those feelings didn't have to stop her holding an ornament. She reached out for it.

The old man behind the counter picked up some more heather but he didn't do anything with it. Instead, he watched the ten-year-old girl closely as she took the pyramid in her right hand and stood it on her left palm. A strange smile came to his lined face when he saw her shiver.

About twenty centimetres high, the three green sides of the pyramid were astonishingly shiny and reminded Nyree of mirrors. Some of the images reflected there seemed close, some far away, none real. The bottom of the pyramid was black and totally unlike a mirror. Light seemed to disappear into the matt surface rather than bounce off it. She had to fight the urge to drop the sculpture when the icy base contacted the skin of her palm.

"What have you found?" Mr Peacock asked her in a

7

voice that sounded too loud. "Not the most decorative, is it?"

"No, but. . ." Nyree muttered without looking up from her hypnotic find.

"But what?"

Nyree had been feeling sick and unsteady but the jade pyramid had distracted her. "This is what I want."

"Really? Are you sure? There's a lot of nicer—"

"I'm sure."

Mr Peacock shrugged. "Take it up to the man, then."

When Nyree walked towards him, the old man stood and nodded knowingly. "That's very special, darling. Most singular." His speech was slow, as if he were not used to the language. He stared into Nyree's face. "I can see why it's chosen you."

Nyree winced as Mr Peacock corrected his faltering grammar. "You mean, why Nyree's chosen it."

"Do I?" the artist retorted without even glancing at Mr Peacock. "Look." He came from behind the counter and took Nyree's arm. Realizing that Nyree's hearing was frail, he spoke up. "This is what you do, darling. Listen. You touch one of the green sides against here." His wrinkled hand went to Nyree's forehead. "Then you put it by your bed, you see, and sleep with a lamp on so the pyramid's shadow falls on you through the night."

Amused, Mr Peacock asked, "And what does that do?"

"That," he answered impatiently, as if an instructor

should have known, "heals the sick."

"How quaint."

"Quaint?" the artist replied, clearly confused and possibly insulted.

Mr Peacock backtracked. "It's. . . er. . . a charming tradition."

The man scowled at him and then turned to Nyree again. "No one touches or disturbs you during pyramid time. You see? Afterwards, you return the pyramid to me. It does not work again. It's like a toy with batteries. Understand? It runs down after a cure. It's yours to use and then it's mine to recharge."

Mr Peacock produced his identity card. "Are you saying we're going to borrow it, not own it?"

The man shook his head and waved away the plastic card. Talking solely to Nyree again, he said, "It's yours, darling. You use it well. But only once and never again. Twice is very dangerous." He wagged a knobbly finger at her and frowned. "Bring it back to me."

"All right," Nyree said quietly, hugging the precious trinket.

"Good," he replied. "You know, I'm glad you came to my trailer."

Nyree didn't know what to reply so she said, "Thank you."

With a wistful expression on his withered face, the old man watched his visitors leave. Then he walked to the window and gazed at Nyree through the filmy glass until she was out of sight.

Back on the walkway, out in the brightness of the real world, Mr Peacock mumbled, "Weird! Different culture altogether. Still, no harm done."

The low sunlight stung Nyree's eyes and brought immediate tears. The hammering in her skull started once more. Even so, she smiled to herself.

For the first time in ages, Nyree felt great. Her head was free of crippling migraine. She didn't feel sore, sick and wobbly. Her vision wasn't flickering and blurred. She walked – almost skipped – out of her own room and in through the forensic investigator's open door. Nyree liked Luke Harding. He was tall and nice and he was bouncing back after the bad guy in his last case had poisoned him. Nyree had her bag over one shoulder and she gripped her shiny pyramid in both hands to guard against dropping it.

"Hey! Look at you," Luke said. "A lot better than when I first saw you. Are you going back to school?"

She nodded, unable to keep a big grin from her face. "I'm better."

"You beat me," Luke replied. "I thought I'd be out before you."

Nyree looked down at her heavy pyramid. "If I gave you this, you'd get well, but. . ." She hugged it to her chest. "I can't."

"It's okay. I'm nearly fit again anyway." Smiling at her, Luke said, "You keep it. If it's a lucky charm, it'll make sure you never have to come back."

"It's made of jade," said Nyree. Thinking of the label on the shelf in that peculiar hut, she added, "And jade's good for you."

Nyree watched as Luke glanced at his other visitor. Maybe she was his girlfriend. Even so, Nyree didn't know why they exchanged a secret smile.

Luke lowered his voice. "That's true. I'll let you into a secret. I've got Jade as well. Saved my life."

Nyree was trying to figure out what he meant when Mr Peacock, lurking at the door, called, "Come on, Nyree. That's enough. Say your goodbyes to the nurses and we can go."

It was the first of March and the annual celebration for the coming to power of The Authorities was in full swing. Robotic clowns with ridiculously long legs and large feet padded along York's riverside walkway, making a variety of synthetic laughing noises. The air was rich with the sulphurous smell of gunpowder and the heady aroma of spices from the barbecue stalls by the bridge. The flashing lights of the colourful fairground rides were reflected in the River Ouse. Firecrackers jumped around, making the sound of gunfire. Every few seconds, a rocket shot into the sky, exploded with the deafening noise of a cannon, and formed a huge vivid mushroom of stars, illuminating the city. At once, the bloom of light began to weep. Sparkling tears of blue and red and yellow and white fell like rain.

Nyree Max stood empty-handed on the river bank. Straining her neck for a while, she watched the big wheel as it rotated slowly, taking sightseers up sixty metres in glass pods. From the top, they'd have fabulous views of the vibrant city bathed in spectacular light. Nyree wasn't going on the wheel because she got jittery with height. Besides, she was fascinated more by the Ouse itself. It had come alive with hundreds of tiny flames. Huge numbers of candles floated gently downstream on small beautiful boats made from leaves. The old man in the riverside shack had probably made quite a few of them.

Most people who pushed out their waterborne candles did it for fun – because it had become tradition. They wanted to see their own mini-boat jostling with all the others, making a stunning display like an unhurried procession of fireflies. A few superstitious people believed that, when they released their candle into the flow, all of their bad luck and ill health would also drift away. Nyree's own candle joined the rest and glided down the river, along with her disabling migraines.

Nyree didn't know if she believed in the supernatural but the pyramid that she'd just taken back to the trailer had worked, so maybe that made her a believer. Unsure, though, she let the question go like a balloon released by a tired child.

By the frequent flashes of light outside his windows, Crawford Gallagher examined the pyramid that the girl had returned. As always when he had to recharge it, he felt queasy. Turning the used pyramid in his shrunken hands, he gazed at the three faces of hard jade. They were an indefinable shade of deep green speckled with the reflections of bright bursts of fireworks. The multicoloured stars glittered in the mirror-like surfaces, but the bottom of the pyramid was different. When Crawford looked at it, he shuddered unpleasantly. No reflections, no light, no life. After a cure, it always appeared to be a hole. He imagined that he could put his hand right into it and feel. . . nothing. He could no more touch the inside of the pyramid than he could reach out on a dark night and touch the infinite sky. Of course, the base wasn't a hole or a tunnel or infinity. It was just a dull surface, used to regenerate the pyramid's healing power.

Carefully, Crawford took the vial of deep red fluid on his counter and unscrewed the cap. Muttering to himself, he said, "I have work for you, my blood brothers." Then he tilted the container over the bottom of the pyramid. The fresh human blood ran out sluggishly and dropped onto that cold surface, giving the jade pyramid fresh life.

Chapter Two

Forensic Investigator Luke Harding had been discharged from York Hospital, but he had not left the complex. Before he'd got anywhere near the main exit, The Authorities had assigned him to an investigation within the hospital. Doing his best to ignore the throbbing ache above his left ear, Luke was circling round a bed in a private treatment room, checking out the male patient who had died there. Luke did not have to test the body to establish the time of death. The bedside monitor had registered the man's last heartbeat three hours and twenty-four minutes previously.

Outside, a war could have been raging. The noise of fireworks sounded like bombs exploding and guns discharging. The flashes could have been missiles crashing into their targets, creating showers of sparks. In the presence of a corpse, Luke was tempted to think of the spectacular celebrations as tactless. But perhaps the dead man would've wanted to leave the world in a blaze of fireworks. Luke had to admit the idea had a certain appeal, unlike death itself. A particularly bright rocket blossomed into blue and white outside the window and distracted Luke. The firework made him think that, after his own death, he'd like his ashes shot into the sky as part of a grand display. It would be even better to have them fired in a real rocket and scattered beyond the atmosphere. That would be the nearest thing to joining the stars.

Luke forced himself to forget the fanciful and concentrate on the squalor of death. He hadn't touched the body. He didn't need to touch it to know that it would be warm and stiffening. He glanced at his Mobile Aid to Law and Crime and said, "Why have I been asked to look into this? He can't be the only patient to die in the hospital. It's bound to happen. The place is full of sick people. What's suspicious about this one?" If it weren't for the patient's uncanny stillness and pale colour, he could have been asleep. There was no sign of blood and no obvious weapon. As death went, this one was pretty. At the age of sixteen, Luke had already seen much worse.

"It is correct that many people die in York Hospital. It has a reputation for treating the most serious illnesses and, as a result, has a high mortality rate. However, The Authorities have noted that the percentage of fatal outcomes began increasing six months ago. You are required to find out if the death statistics are caused by worsening illnesses, medical mistakes or criminal activity."

The blast of a giant firework shook the window. Luke took a deep breath. "What's his name and how old was he?"

"Julian Bent, aged forty-two years and three months."

Luke stooped down to examine the patient's exposed right arm. "A lot of pricks here. I guess the hospital fed him via a drip and took blood samples. But it means anybody could inject him with a poison and no one would be any wiser."

"Do you wish the pathologist to carry out toxicology tests?" asked Malc.

"Sure do. And I want all his medicines and drips analysed. I want to know if they're what they're supposed to be and not laced with anything nasty."

"Transmitting tasks."

"Why was he in here? What was wrong with him?"

"He had cancer of the pancreas."

Luke said, "What did the doctor make of his death?"

"It was considered sudden but within normal parameters for an acute pancreatic tumour. Such patients can deteriorate quickly, before the cancer can be removed surgically. In this case, the operation would have been difficult and the cancer might have already spread. The patient was classified as terminal."

Luke stopped prowling around and looked over the bed at the door. "I didn't need an identity card to get in here."

"Correct. That is the hospital's policy. Patients' doors are not locked, enabling immediate access by medical teams in an emergency."

"So, anyone disguised in a white coat could wander in,

and there's no record of who's come and gone."

"Confirmed. It is reasonable to assume that several members of the hospital staff and an unknown number of visitors will have entered these quarters recently."

Luke sighed. "Maybe not a cleaner, though. Look. What's this on the floor?" He pointed at a small fragment of a plant with dark green spiky foliage and a tiny ruby petal.

Malc scanned it and then compared it with his wildlife database. "It is part of a heather called *Erica carnea*."

"Is it poisonous?"

"No."

Luke nodded. "Okay. Someone probably gave him a bunch of flowers, that's all." Finely tuned to unusual traces, he added, "There's a small feather sticking to the end of the blanket."

"It matches the plume of a juvenile duck. A DNA analysis should confirm it, if required."

"Mmm. What about these crumbs, Malc?" He pointed to several small brown specks on the bedside table.

"They are fragments of a biscuit."

"What sort?"

"They consist of oats, desiccated coconut and linseed but they do not match any entries in my database of commercial biscuits."

"Perhaps they're homemade. Scan the whole room, then call the agents in. I can't have the place sealed because another patient will need it, so I want them to bag everything up. The bed sheets, that bit of heather and any hairs, fibres, specks of skin, the lot – in case I need to analyse them later. Then get the pathologist on the job. Let's get those tests done on the body."

"Transmitting."

"And I suppose you're going to tell me I've got to swing into action every time someone dies in the hospital."

"No. It is unnecessary to tell you what you already know."

Not yet back to full strength, Luke groaned. "I'm going to be busy."

The ward supervisor seemed irritable, probably because she thought Luke was questioning her competence and the conduct of her staff. She glanced up at the ceiling, calming herself, before she answered. "Yes. I think I can tell you which staff attended Julian Bent. Most of them anyway."

"Doctors, nurses and other staff. Like cleaners."

"Yes," she muttered.

"And visitors. If you could make a list on your computer, Malc can download it."

The ward supervisor curled her lip at the thought of the extra effort. "I don't know about visitors but I'll ask my nurses, I suppose. His partner came in now and again.

That I do know."

"Thanks. You've locked away his medication and drips, haven't you?"

She nodded.

"Good. Some agents will come and get them to do a few tests. Just one more thing. Was anything disturbed in his room?"

She frowned. "No, I don't think so."

Shrugging, Luke said, "It doesn't really matter, but I was wondering who took the flowers out."

The ward supervisor frowned again. "Flowers? He didn't have any as far as I know."

The fireworks had come to an end, most of the revellers had gone home, and the night had fallen into a hush. Luke lay on the hotel bed, unable to sleep. He gazed at the stars that his mobile had projected onto the ceiling and said, "Sharpen the image a bit, Malc. It looks fuzzy to me."

"You are incorrect," Malc replied. "It is perfectly focused."

Luke rubbed his eyes. "Must be me, then."

"You cannot expect complete recovery from your injuries in one week."

"You've got a lovely bedside manner," Luke said with a weak smile. "Almost as if you cared."

"I am programmed to protect you. That includes monitoring your recovery from illness."

"If York's got worse death statistics than other hospitals, there must be something different about it. Maybe it's a rogue member of staff. Compare databases, Malc. Make a list of recruits who joined the hospital at the same time as the death rate started to go up. That'd be around September. And check if any of them has got a criminal record. What else? If any came from another health centre to work here, check if the percentage of deaths went down as soon as they left their last place."

"Processing. This task will take several minutes."

"Okay. Is there anything else unusual about York Hospital?"

"It is a Tuition and Research Hospital."

"So, there are students practising and trials of experimental treatments."

"Correct."

"Mmm. Is that all?" Luke asked.

"It has four specialized centres. You know about the poisoning unit because it cured you. The second is a Phobia Clinic."

"For people who're scared of things like slugs?"

"Correct," Malc answered. "It also carries out research into stress hormones associated with irrational fears."

"All my fears are rational," Luke said. "Like being scared of an axe coming in my direction. Anyway, what's next?"

"It has an Institute of Biomechanical Research where

specialist engineers test how human organs and tissues behave under pressure. Current projects include studying injuries caused by bullets, bombs and other sudden impacts."

"And the last thing?"

"It has a Department of Alternative Medicine."

"What does that do?"

"It uses natural remedies, acupuncture, homeopathy, hypnosis, chiropractic and other unconventional therapies that currently defy explanation, and it conducts scientific investigations into their effectiveness and mode of action."

"Interesting. Who's in charge?"

"The chief consultant is Peter Sachs."

Abruptly, Luke gasped and twisted his head towards Malc. Ignoring the pain in his neck, he cried, "Who?"

"Dr Peter Sachs."

Luke's body was tingling all over. "Run me a check on that name, Malc. Top priority. Is there more than one doctor called Peter Sachs in the country?"

Malc delayed his other remote searches. After two minutes, he answered, "No."

Luke looked back at the artificial sky. Lost in thought, he muttered, "It must be the Peter Sachs I know, then."

"Confirmed," Malc replied. "I have consulted his files." Without a trace of sentiment, the mobile reported, "He is your father."

Chapter Three

When Peter Sachs had been a young doctor, he'd been paired with the astronomer, Elisa Harding, and they'd had their quota of two children. As Luke approached the age of five, Peter and Elisa had prepared to hand him over to Birmingham School, as the law required. A child was a brief blessing, not the parents' possession. The Authorities insisted that school-age children had to have freedom to develop in their own way and parents needed freedom to further their careers. Luke's little sister, Kerryanne Harding, would have followed his lead, but she'd lost her fight against disease before either of them had enrolled at school.

That painful time with Kerryanne was Luke's last recollection of his family. On the verge of going to school, he remembered his mother's misery and his father's anger. Peter Sachs would have been furious with himself because a doctor should have had the ability to cure his own daughter. When she died, he must have thought that he'd let her down at an absurdly young age. Even though the law allowed Peter and Elisa to compensate for Kerryanne's loss, they had never had another child.

The Authorities had cared for Luke adequately since the age of five, as they cared for all children once their parents had delivered them to school. Most young people seemed satisfied with the arrangement, but Luke felt that something was missing. He wasn't sure what it was, but he wondered if his parents would have provided it if he'd had longer with them. That missing element was one reason why Luke had always had a secret wish to meet his parents again. He imagined standing in front of them, spreading his arms and saying, "It's me. This is how I turned out." He liked to think that they'd be proud of him. But he'd never got around to asking Malc to trace them. Until today, he'd had no idea if they were still alive or where they were.

Now a reunion with his parents was no longer a distant dream. Luke even had an excuse to talk to his father. He could go and conduct an interview right away. But he didn't move from his bed. He stared at the blurred stars and decided that he couldn't. Not yet. It was all too sudden. He wasn't ready.

Interrupting Luke's thoughts, Malc announced, "I have a list of fourteen people employed by York Hospital since the time of the increase in fatalities. None has a criminal record. Eleven moved from other health centres. I find no evidence of a decrease in fatality rates at their previous places of employment, suggesting that none of them has caused deaths before."

"Anything from the pathologist yet?"

"No," Malc answered.

"Has the analytical lab got any results?"

"Confirmed. No contamination has been detected in the patient's medication, nutrition or saline solution."

"Okay," Luke said, his eyes still fixed on his personal planetarium. "Try something else. Search for anything common to all recent deaths. I mean, were a lot of them on the same medicine, suffering the same disease, treated by the same doctor, or in the same drug trial? Something like that."

"Task logged. However, you should note that it may be impossible to recognize trends among the few extra deaths when they are mixed in with a large majority of natural fatalities."

Luke replied, "Use your imagination, Malc."

"I don't have—"

Interrupting his mobile, Luke said, "See if you can distinguish the extra deaths from the ones that would have happened anyway. How many have there been?"

"Since September, twenty-seven more patients have died than the hospital's six-monthly average."

"Twenty-seven," Luke replied. "Okay. Look for something else that's gone up by twenty to thirty in the past six months. If it's terminal cancer cases or heart attacks, my job's done. It's just that people are sicker. If twenty-odd patients had the same experimental treatment, it looks like a medical mistake. Probably a dodgy drug. You get my drift."

"I recognize the statistical analysis that you require. However, even if such a correlation existed, you would have to verify cause and effect. Otherwise, it could be coincidence."

"Well, the sooner you do your sums, the sooner I'll have data to play with."

Luke's last case had left him with more than a headache and slightly blurred vision. He fingered the stitched gashes in his cheek and neck while he waited for Malc to sift through the hospital's files. With ill health on his mind, he thought of his sister. He didn't know how Kerryanne had died. He could remember only that she'd suffered a disease rather than an accident or crime.

Malc announced, "I have downloaded a list of the hospital staff attending to Julian Bent, and the patient's one known visitor."

"Was that his wife?"

"Confirmed. Her name is Romilly Dando."

"Someone to interview tomorrow, then. Set it up, please, Malc."

"Logged for processing when I have spare resource."

Luke was used to thinking of DNA as an aid to an investigation. Now he lay back and thought about it as a recipe for making him what he was. He'd inherited his genes from his mother and father, from an astronomer and a doctor. That's why he'd become a forensic investigator. He'd been given the curiosity and techniques of a scientist, and a devotion to people's welfare. Maybe it was his share of Elisa Harding's genes that made him sprawl on the bed and take comfort from the stars. Mostly, though, he and his mother worked at opposite ends of a telescope. She looked for massive objects in the huge expanse of outer space while he poked around for the tiniest traces in a confined space. Yet they were both searching for evidence of past events. They both had mysteries to unravel. Luke felt a great affinity with the mother he hardly knew.

"I have completed the attempt to distinguish recent excess deaths by linking to common factors."

"And?"

"I have not completed any other tasks at this time," Malc replied.

"No. I mean, what have you found?"

"There are two correlations that may be significant. Of all deceased patients in York Hospital since September, twenty-four more than normal had organs removed for transplant."

Luke turned towards Malc and grimaced. "Now, that's a motive I wouldn't have thought of, if you're thinking what I'm thinking."

"I do not know what you are thinking and, strictly speaking, I do not think at all."

Luke smiled. "The motive is, people might've been killed to provide human organs for transplant. Nasty."

"Insufficient data, but it is valid speculation. Such an activity has never been reported in this country. However, one overseas state has been accused of executing certain criminals quickly to address specific organ shortages. It is likely that prisoners are selected for the death penalty not on the basis of their crimes but by their blood groups and tissue compatibility with people requiring transplants. The fact that there are transplant units in their high-security prisons is consistent with the accusation. In addition, their cosmetics industry has been prosecuted for harvesting skin from executed criminals and using it to develop anti-ageing and beauty products. It is argued that organs and skin have been harvested without prior consent of the prisoners, which is against international law."

"Harvesting sounds nicer than nicking body parts, doesn't it? But I'll have to think about it as a motive, with hospital patients instead of prisoners. What's the second connection?"

"Twenty-six patients have died while taking part in clinical trials of unconventional treatments."

Luke inhaled deeply and then let the long breath go. "That means I need to talk to Peter Sachs."

"That is the recommended action."

"Don't set an interview up, Malc. I want to do it in my own time."

Luke gazed at the stars until his tired eyes would stay

open no longer.

Romilly Dando was leaning against the wall next to the window, looking absently out at her ranch in the Heslington area of York. In front of her was an artificial lake. It was the centrepiece of her fish and duck farm. Everywhere around the water's edge, there were groups of ducks and the walkways were awash with their droppings. To the right, a helper was chopping wood frenziedly with an axe. He seemed to be taking out some unknown frustration on the logs.

Romilly barely looked at Luke when he introduced himself. She nodded towards the view of the ranch and muttered, "All this is mine now. It'll never be the same." She shook her head miserably.

"Julian ran it with you, did he?"

"Yes."

"I'm sorry," Luke said. "I've got to ask you some questions." But he already had an explanation for the presence of a feather from a young duck in Julian's room.

Romilly didn't shift from the window. She just leaned her head on the frame. "I blame the pesticides, fertilisers and all."

"Is that what the hospital said? Cancer caused by agricultural chemicals?"

"They didn't say anything about causes. They just went through the usual treatments. Not that it did any good."

Luke asked, "Did they try any unusual treatments?"

At last, Romilly glanced at him. "What do you mean?"

"Did they suggest anything new, experimental or unconventional?"

"Not to tackle the cancer. Not as far as I know. They tried acupuncture to help with the pain."

"Were you with him when he. . ."

Romilly sniffed, trying to keep her composure. "No. It happened too quickly."

"Sorry to ask this, but did he – or you – give the hospital permission to remove any organs for transplant?"

"Someone mentioned something like that but. . . Would they want anything with the cancer and all? Anyway, I didn't want him to be. . . messed with."

"Did he have any other visitors, do you know?"

Outside, two ducks quacked loudly at each other and then started a fight. Romilly turned towards her visitor. "Why are you asking me all this?"

Luke shrugged. "It's just routine. You know. To make sure everything's being done properly."

Julian's partner switched her gaze back to the lake. "No, I think I was the only one. He wasn't even keen for me to see him suffering like that, and all."

"Did you visit anyone else in the hospital while you were there?"

She sighed. "No. Just Julian."

"By the way, did you bake him any biscuits?"

"No. He liked them, though." Keeping her eyes averted from Luke, she added, "I should've done."

"Did you – or anyone else – give him heather?"

"Heather? No. He wouldn't have liked that. He didn't want a fuss."

Chapter Four

The pathologist's report did not cast any extra light on Julian Bent's death. There were no suspicious circumstances and the cause of death was rampant cancer. Luke listened to Malc's emotionless reading of the pathologist's conclusions and watched the outskirts of York slip past. "You know," he said, "Julian Bent might not have been the best place to start this case. Everything's telling me it's natural. Cruel, but natural."

The automatic cab was racing north towards Malton and Luke's heart was thudding. Malc had found that Peter Sachs and Elisa Harding were now living in the small market town. The astronomer was at work but the doctor was having a rare day off from his hospital duties. Luke was only a few minutes away from meeting his father again.

"Just one thing," said Luke. "Were there acupuncture holes in his skin — or at least marks where they'd healed over?"

"No."

Luke frowned. "Strange."

The area around Malton was dedicated to growing corn. Right now, the farmland was bare, but two auto-vehicles were trundling to and fro, sowing seeds. As the electric cab slowed for the approach to the town, Luke caught sight of horses galloping around a field on his left. A trainer with both hands round his mouth was shouting instructions to the jockeys. Beyond them was the River Derwent.

Luke let Malc guide him towards Peter and Elisa's house because his mobile was equipped with a detailed map of the entire country. Even though Luke didn't know the way, it felt a little like going home because he didn't have his own fixed address. He simply went wherever crime took him. "Just a minute," he said to Malc. He paused by the river and, for a while, watched the Derwent surging past. He was not sure if he was looking forward to the coming interview or not. Of course, it was much more than an interview for Luke. He took some deep breaths, trying to steady his nerves and control his excitement.

"Your minute has elapsed," Malc informed him.

"Yeah, all right. Let's get going."

Malc led him to a small cottage, not a state-of-the-art apartment. Clearly, his parents had taken a step back after he'd gone to school. At the side of the cottage, a man in a padded jacket was sitting at an easel, painting. Straight away, Luke recognized an aged version of his father. Luke hesitated, swallowed nervously and then walked up to him without a word.

The sunshine coming over Luke's shoulder made Peter squint at his visitor. There was no sign of recognition in his eyes. "Yes?" he prompted.

Why should his father realize who he was? He'd last seen his son eleven years ago, at the age of five. Very deliberately, Luke extracted his identity card and held it out. "Er. . . Forensic Investigator Luke Harding," he announced.

For a few seconds, Peter was dumbstruck. Then his mouth opened. "But. . ." His eyes flicked again between the card and Luke's face. "I'm. . ."

It was clear in his father's moist eyes that he was overcome. But there was also the beginning of a smile on his face.

Peter looked Luke up and down. Then he glanced down at his fingers. "Sorry. I'm covered in paint." He wiped his hands clumsily and hurriedly on a cloth, then stood and held out his arms. Hugging Luke fiercely, he said into his ear, "Hello, Son. It's good to see you."

It seemed to Luke that his father accepted him immediately and unconditionally. Taken by surprise, he whispered back, "Hello, Father."

Luke did not match his father in facial features but both of them were tall and had the same build.

Peter pulled back and held Luke's shoulders at arm's length. "You'd look great if it weren't for. . ." The doctor peered at the gash in Luke's cheek. "Whatever you've been doing, someone's patched you up well. You won't have much of a scar. Not an ugly one. The Authorities must be looking after you."

Luke didn't want to talk about his injuries. That would've been a wasted opportunity. Instead, he looked at his father's unfinished artwork. It featured two sinewy racehorses. Nodding at it, he said, "Unusual."

"Not round here. It's a centre for horse training."

"No," Luke said, "I meant, unusual for a doctor to paint."

Peter smiled. "That's what The Authorities teach us all, isn't it? We're supposed to become expert at one thing and stick to it, but. . . I paint to relax. Do you always do what The Authorities tell you?"

Luke had been warned to stop using unorthodox methods and to heed Malc's advice at all times. He'd also been cautioned over his opposition to pairing. "Um, nearly always," he answered coyly.

Peter laughed happily. "Nearly means no. Excellent. That's my legacy to you."

"What?"

"A healthy scepticism."

Luke nodded. He liked the idea of having a rebellious father.

"You got good looks from your mother and a questioning mind from me." Peter hesitated before adding proudly, "And your own efforts made you the country's youngest FI."

Luke was taken aback. "How do you know that?"

Peter smiled at him. "Did you think we'd lose track altogether, me and your mother? Did you think we wouldn't be interested? We've been hoping you'd get in touch. We knew you would one day. Let's go in." Heading for the back door, he led the way down a path and past a greenhouse.

"How's Mother?" asked Luke.

"She's up at Fylingdales – North York Moors Observatory – still gazing at stars for a living." He looked into Luke's face and said, "She'll be home soon. She'll be pleased to see you, to say the least. Like discovering a new planet, but. . ." For an instant, his expression darkened. Then he stripped off his coat, brushed a bit of dandruff from its collar, and waved Luke towards a seat. "What do you want to drink? Pomegranate juice? Or something stronger, maybe a tiny bit illegal?"

"Just pomegranate juice, thanks."

Peter grinned. "When you were little you wanted so much of the stuff, I almost gave you an intravenous drip."

Bracing himself, Luke said, "I'm not sure I'm really ready for this get-together in the way you meant it. I've come to see you, for sure, but I'm on a case. Sorry. I need to ask you about the hospital."

Peter nodded, trying not to look disappointed. "I'll get us that drink. I'll put a drop of something in it to give it a kick. Sounds like we're going to need it."

Chapter Five

When Peter returned to the compact living room with a glass in each hand, still stained colourfully with dried paint, he said, "I can't get over. . . anyway, let's get the business done, before your mother gets back." He gulped down a large part of the juice.

"Are there any medicines based on heather?" Luke asked.

"Not that I'm aware of, but some people say it brings good luck. Rubbish, of course. But you've told me you found out what I do, just like I found out what you do."

"Chief Consultant of the Department of Alternative Medicine." Luke sipped the pomegranate juice and found that it did have a kick. A pleasant, warming kick. He didn't ask what was in it, though, because Malc would probably report Peter to The Authorities if it was prohibited.

"You know what I do but I'd better tell you why."

"Oh?"

That cloud came over his features again. "It. . . er. . . it goes back to Kerryanne. I don't know what you remember, but. . . sickness is bad enough when it strikes down the old. It's absolutely hateful when it afflicts the young." He bowed his head. "I couldn't save her. Modern medicine couldn't save her."

"What did she have?"

"It started with headaches that wouldn't go away. Then came poor eyesight, nausea and vomiting. She went deaf and got terribly confused." Peter finished off his drink as if he were parched. "It was a brain tumour. A rapidly growing medulloblastoma. She saw a hundred and one specialists, had a hundred and one scans and X-rays, every medication going. And she hardly ever complained. A couple of operations proved only the tumour was inoperable. She went through everything that conventional medicine could throw at her, but it was useless. Nothing loosened the cancer's grip." He put his head in his hands briefly and then looked up again, but he didn't make eye contact with Luke. "She was discharged from hospital because she'd exhausted every option. She died a few weeks later. You see, modern medicine can't solve everything. That's why I looked around for something extra. That's why I set up an alternative-medicine unit."

"I remember being outside with her – and you – one night. Under the stars. Wrapped in a blanket. She held my hand."

A single tear ran down Peter's cheek. "That was your mother's idea – to make her last night special. We knew we were going to lose her the next day. She died with dignity."

Lost for words, Luke nodded.

37

"I'd better tell you. . ." Peter continued. "But do you want another drink first?"

Luke shook his head. "Still got plenty."

Peter got up. "I need another one." When he returned with a full glass, he said, "It's not just physical wounds that leave a scar. Me and your mother, we never really recovered. Do you know what I mean? We'd been happy, but after Kerryanne. . ." He sighed deeply. "I blamed myself because I was a doctor, and your mother. . ." He ground to a halt.

"What?" Luke asked softly.

"The tumour was left over from nerve cells that didn't develop properly while Kerryanne was growing inside your mother. Because it was something that happened inside her, Elisa blamed herself. That's why we never had another baby – in case she inflicted the same thing on another child."

Luke nodded again. It all made sense now.

Plainly, Peter couldn't take any more. He needed to talk about something else for a while. He said, "It's not about mystical nonsense, you understand. My department, that is. It studies natural remedies and things like that, scientifically."

"Including acupuncture."

"Yes. The science isn't convincing, but we know acupuncture releases natural painkillers from the brain. It can help with nausea and some chronic pain. But don't get bogged down with one branch. I'll fill you in on the bigger picture." He took a moment to think, and then said, "There's conventional medicine and what I do. The difference isn't always obvious when you look at cures. A herb with an active ingredient sounds alternative but a lot of conventional drugs come from trees and plants, even aspirin. But there's a big difference in approach. Conventional medicine says the body's a big machine with lots of parts that can go wrong. It's all about fixing the bits that break down. My department's not like that. We think of the body as a whole, not a collection of parts, and illness is when the entire network goes out of balance. It's all about problems with the relationships between interacting systems, not just the breakdown of one cog in a machine. Think of a body as a self-regulating network that gets itself in a twist sometimes and settles in the wrong place. We aim to treat the whole thing, not fix the bits. In fact, we don't really aim for a cure as such. The network's too complicated for that. We just disturb the balance – nudge the system – and let it settle in the right place. Sometimes we're successful, sometimes not. We always do it scientifically, though. It's not magic."

"Did you treat someone called Julian Bent?"

His father shrugged. "The name's vaguely familiar, but I can't keep track of everyone."

"I'm checking it out because the hospital's death rate has gone up."

"That's because we're taking on trickier cases, I guess. Tougher diseases, more deaths."

"My job's to prove that, or come up with the real reason." Luke took another sip. He couldn't delay any more. He had to throw some suspicion on his father's unit. "About twenty-seven more patients than normal have died. It might be coincidence but twenty-six people in your trials of alternative treatments have died."

Peter did not look surprised. "I know. I keep my eye on statistics as well. I've already checked them out as much as I can. The fact is, they were in four totally different trials and they weren't getting any treatment anyway so it couldn't have been a trial going wrong."

Luke was puzzled. "Oh? How come they didn't get anything?"

"They were what we call controls. They thought they were guinea pigs for an experimental remedy but actually they were getting only placebos. That means dummy treatments. We've got to have controls to compare with patients who are getting the real remedies."

"So, a dodgy new drug didn't kill them, but your cures must've looked pretty impressive when they died. People carry on living if they're getting the experimental treatment and die if they don't."

"True," Peter admitted. He leaned forward towards his son. "But what are you saying? Having a placebo is a motive for murder? That's an extreme way of improving our statistics. And impossible."

"Impossible?"

"My medical team doesn't know who's getting the genuine treatment and who's getting the dummy. Neither do the patients."

"Someone must know," Luke said, "or you wouldn't be able to work the results out afterwards."

"Yes, but she's not part of my medical team. She doesn't have an interest in the success or failure of a treatment. Deliberately. She's a young mathematician and she's the only one who knows who gets what. I give her twenty names and say, 'Put ten people on a test remedy and ten on placebos,' and she gets on with it. She assigns each name to a remedy or placebo at random. It's called double-blind because the patients and the medical team are blind to who gets what. Not even I know until the trial's over."

"What's her name? This mathematician."

"Tara Fortune."

"When did she start work with you?" Luke asked.

"I don't know. Hospital files will tell you. I guess it was about six months ago."

Luke and Peter exchanged a glance when they heard footsteps approaching the house. Standing up, they both faced the front door and waited.

Chapter Six

Elisa Harding walked into the living room. For a moment, she was startled to see two people. Then a look of delight came to her face. "Luke!" she cried. "It's you!"

Unable to keep a babyish grin from his face, Luke found himself in another enthusiastic embrace. "How did you know?" he asked her. "It's been eleven years."

His mother pretended to be insulted. "Are you trying to tell me I can't recognize my own son, no matter how long it's been? Hey, you're tall."

"Taller than the last time you saw me."

Elisa was so mesmerized by Luke's appearance, she forgot to laugh. She didn't greet Peter or even smile at him. Maybe she ignored her partner because she couldn't take her eyes off Luke. Maybe it was the effect of familiarity. Or maybe there was another reason. She nodded towards Luke's cheek and said, "You've been in the wars."

"Just got thwacked by a branch." Luke wasn't entirely truthful because he thought she might worry if he told her that a falling tree was a deliberate attempt on his life.

"It's still a dangerous job." Elisa frowned at him.

"It's okay. And Malc looks after me." He jerked his thumb towards his mobile.

His mother said, "I heard about you on the news."

"Oh?"

"They said you were investigating the Emily Wonder murders."

"Oh, yes. That was one of mine."

"You solved it." Elisa oozed satisfaction and pride.

Malc did not distinguish between a social chat and an interview. "Forensic Investigator Luke Harding has a one hundred per cent clear-up record," he reported. There was no pride in Malc's tone. He was simply supplying a fact.

"That's brilliant," Elisa said to Luke. "And exactly what I'd expect." Then she changed the subject. "You'll stay for dinner." It was not quite a question, almost a demand. "And we've got a spare bed. We've got a lot to catch up on." She glanced at Luke's mobile and added, "You know, for some reason, I expected you to bring a girl, not a tin machine."

At once, Malc objected. "I am made from an advanced alloy that—"

Luke smiled and said, "Silent mode, Malc." Then he turned back to his mother. "Funny you should say that. I always imagined bringing. . ."

Elisa still hadn't taken her coat off. "So, there is a girl. Are you going to be paired? What's her name?"

"Jade Vernon."

His mother hesitated. "Why do I know. . .?"

At last, Peter intervened. "I see," he said thoughtfully.

Impatiently, Elisa asked him, "What do you see?"

"She's the musician doing the anthem for the International Youth Games. We've seen her on the telescreen."

Luke nodded. "She's also my girlfriend. Has been for ages. She saved my life."

For a moment, neither of his parents spoke. They didn't have to. Luke knew what they were thinking. A musician would not be paired with a forensic investigator because The Authorities formed couples on the basis of career, genetics, age and intelligence. Luke's parents were regretting that he'd fallen for the wrong girl.

Luke gazed at his father and said with a smile, "That's your legacy coming out in me. A healthy scepticism for pairing."

Peter thought about it before nodding. "Good for you. She looked nice."

Elisa stared at her partner as if he'd trivialized an important issue.

Peter knocked back more of his drink. "Have faith," he said to her. "Luke will figure it out. He's got a one hundred per cent record."

Over the meal, Luke almost forgot his persistent headache. He talked about himself, about his job, Malc, Jade and her music. He watched his father drink a large volume of the juice with a kick and his mother ignore her husband. It was odd that these damaged people he didn't know had taken to him at once. He got the impression that they would have supported him through success and failure, through good times and bad. He was troubled that his case required him to regard his father as a potential suspect.

Luke's role of forensic investigator was never far from his mind. Thinking of Nyree Max, the gaunt girl with the lucky charm, he said to his father, "This'll sound a bit silly, but have you ever heard of a pyramid being used to make people better?"

"A pyramid? No. I haven't come across that. There's a superstition about living in the shadow of a pyramid. It's supposed to be good luck. I think that's why some city centres have got a tower-block in the shape of a pyramid but. . ." He shrugged.

"You haven't heard of it in health?"

"Architecture, maybe. Health, no. Superstitions comfort people who believe in them, of course, so they make some patients feel better. No doubt about that." He wasn't making fun of the superstitious. Rather, he seemed to think they had an advantage over everyone else.

"There's something else," Luke said. "Placebos. I see how you could give someone a dummy pill and make them think they're getting the real thing, but how do you do placebo acupuncture?"

Peter smiled. "Good question. It sounds impossible,

doesn't it? But it isn't. We've invented a mimic needle. You put a sheath on the patient's skin and feed the needle down it so they think it's real, but it isn't. It's too blunt to pierce skin, but it feels like it does. Very realistic. It's all in the design of the tip. Because of the sheath, patients can't see it hasn't gone in."

That, thought Luke, explained why Romilly believed Julian had had acupuncture but the pathologist didn't find any sign of it.

Later, when Luke was sitting in the tiny spare bedroom on his own with the lamp off, the door began to open silently. Before anyone could enter, Malc flung himself in front of Luke, his laser primed.

Framed in light from the hall, Elisa appeared in the doorway, holding a box in both hands as if it were precious. "Luke?"

"Yes?" Talking to his mobile, Luke said, "Relax, Malc."

"Your father's drunk himself to sleep. Again. Still punishing himself, punishing us both. Can I come in?"

"Sure."

Elisa switched on the lamp. "I want to share something with you." She placed the container on the bed and carefully removed the lid. "It's a memory box."

Luke blinked repeatedly in the sudden brightness. "A what?"

"Kerryanne's memory box. Look." She removed a soft woollen toy in the shape of a dolphin. "Her favourite. She used to sleep with it." Elisa lifted the toy to her nose and breathed in. "Sometimes, I think I can still smell her." She put the dolphin on the blanket. "I don't suppose you remember." She took a clear plastic envelope between her forefinger and thumb. "A lock of her hair. Part of what fell out."

It was like an evidence bag. Of course, it was an evidence bag in a way. It was evidence that Kerryanne had lived.

There was a hairbrush, a magnifying glass and her favourite dress. Elisa held up the green garment and whispered, "So small."

"Sorry, Mother."

Lovingly, Elisa folded the dress and replaced it in the box. "And this." She held up an old memory stick. "Photographs. Can your machine take a copy?"

"Yes."

"Do you want them?"

"I don't know," Luke replied. "Yes. I think so." He turned to Malc and said, "Download them, please."

"It is obsolete technology but I can connect remotely and convert the data to a modern format."

"Okay," Luke said. "Do it."

Elisa put her hand on her son's knee. "When I think of her, I think of a planet that used to orbit between Mars and Jupiter. A long time ago, gravitational changes nudged it off course. No one knows exactly what

47

happened to it. It could've flown out of the solar system or it might've hurtled into the sun. It's either still out there, all alone on an infinite journey in empty space, or it's burnt up."

Sitting beside his mother, Luke felt like a child again, not a sixteen-year-old professional. He put an arm lightly around her shoulders. "It's not your fault, you know."

She ignored his comment. "You don't get headaches, do you?"

She looked so fearful that Luke lied again. "No." To distract his mother, he said, "Now I want to show you something." He turned to his mobile. "Malc, project the usual image onto the ceiling, please."

Luke watched his mother's face as she looked up at the artificial night sky that always entranced him as he went to sleep. Her lips curved into a faint smile and she nodded. But his tactic failed to distract her from Kerryanne.

"That's something else I think about," she said, still surveying the ceiling. "The sun's got a sibling. Did you know? It's called HD98618 – not the prettiest name, is it? Twenty-six thousand light years away from the centre of the Milky Way and just like our sun. It's got the same elements and it's only one percent hotter, making it five hundred million years younger than our sun. That's almost nothing in astronomy. It's so similar, it could have planets like the Earth. Our sun – sun with a "u", I mean – keeps us alive, but its sister's so far away we can't even find out if it supports life." She twisted her neck to look into Luke's face. "Don't mind me. I'm just a silly emotional astronomer."

"What was Kerryanne like?"

Elisa tapped the magnifying glass and said, "Just like you. Curious about everything. Another little star." She paused before adding, "She was this dazzling creature, trapped inside a broken body. It hid the real Kerryanne. She was brave and cheerful and tough. You know, she refused to wear the wig we thought would look nice. She wanted to face the world exactly as she was. She was right. Thinking back, we probably pushed the wig at her to make us feel more comfortable when we looked at her. It wasn't really for her benefit, even though we told her it was." Elisa took a deep breath. "I watched a lot of sport – sprinters, weight-lifters, rowers, the lot – and not one of them could match Kerryanne's strength."

Elisa looked up again as if she were trying to pick out the star named HD98618.

Chapter Seven

Sharing a cab to York Hospital in the morning, Luke and Peter talked about music, sport, news, computers, telescreen programmes, even the weather. Anything as long as it wasn't murder. Nearing York, the corridor ran alongside the busy canal. The waterway was choked with auto-barges bringing goods to the heart of the city. Narrow boats going in the other direction would be carrying shipments of York's renowned chocolate, glass and sophisticated fireworks.

About to go their separate ways at the hospital terminus, Luke and Peter both knew they couldn't put it off any longer. Peter gazed into his son's face and asked, "Am I a murder suspect?"

Feeling embarrassed, Luke said, "Malc. You answer that, please."

The mobile replied, "You have not yet proved that any of the excess fatalities at York Hospital were the result of murder. However, if there are cases of unlawful killing, Dr Sachs has the medical knowledge and opportunity required to commit such crimes because he works at the hospital. Also, he has a motive because casualties among his control group appear to improve the results of his unconventional treatments."

Knowing that he would fail, Luke tried to defend his

father against Malc's ruthless reasoning. "It's totally against the doctors' code of conduct. 'Do no harm' is their first rule. So, is it likely that a doctor would kill?"

"Unknown. However, you should consider the possibility that the death of the suspect's daughter disturbed the balance of his mind. In addition, there are several precedents. In Manchester—"

"All right," Luke said to silence his mobile. Then he turned to his father. "Sorry."

Peter smiled wryly and scratched his itchy scalp. "I can't fault the logic."

Luke tried to lighten the mood. "You're not the only one to get on his wrong side. He told me I was the main suspect in my first case. Came close to asking me to arrest myself. He's good at logic, hopeless at common sense."

Resigned to being a suspect, Peter nodded. "I guess you might need to talk to me again as an FI. But you'll come back and see us socially, won't you? We won't have to wait till one of us goes on another crime spree, will we?"

Luke glanced at Malc and said, "That was sarcasm, not a confession." Turning back to his father, Luke shook his head. "Can't be too careful with Malc. But, no. I'd like that. Maybe I could bring Jade. . ."

"Good idea. It'd be good to get to know her."

Peter shook Luke's hand awkwardly and then headed

for the Department of Alternative Medicine. Luke was called to Accidents and Emergency.

A lifeless four-year-old girl had just been brought into the hospital and she had failed to respond to resuscitation. She'd been pronounced dead only minutes before Luke reached her room.

Outside it, two nurses were holding back the girl's distraught mother. She was sobbing and shouting in turns. "She's my daughter! I've got to see her. You can't. . ."

The ward supervisor tried to talk calmly to her. "I'm sorry but we've got an emergency procedure. . ."

"Procedure!"

Luke hesitated by the door, touched by the woman's distress.

"Why's he going in?" she shouted accusingly, yanking her arms in an attempt to break free of the nurses. "He doesn't even know Alexia."

"That's the procedure I was telling you about," the harassed supervisor said, trying to reason with her. "At the moment, an investigator's got to be first to see any patients who've passed away."

The girl's mother stared at Luke and swore at the top of her voice.

For a moment, Luke imagined his own mother, distraught at Kerryanne's death. "It's all right," he said to the ward supervisor. "She can go in. I'll wait."

At once, Malc objected. "That is against The Authorities' instructions. You are required to attend each scene at the earliest opportunity, before it is contaminated."

"I am also required to be human, Malc. I'm letting her go in. End of argument." He looked at the mother and said, "I'm sorry. You go and do what you have to. But my mobile will come in with you. He'll stay well back, out of your way. He won't say anything. Okay?"

Her face seemed to be dissolving in grief. "Just let me in!" she cried.

Luke nodded towards the nurses.

As soon as the door closed behind the grieving mother and Malc, the ward supervisor said, "That was a nice gesture but. . ."

"What?" asked Luke.

"It might've been a mistake. We know all about Wendy Ridge. This time it looks like she's gone too far."

Luke frowned. "How do you mean?"

Lowering her voice, the ward supervisor said, "Have you heard of Munchausen's Syndrome by Proxy? We're not sure, but Wendy's doctor reckons she's got it. It started when she brought Alexia in for no reason. Over and over again. She made symptoms up just to get the girl hospital attention. Then it got more. . . sinister. Alexia did get ill, but her mother was probably causing it."

"Why?"

The ward supervisor shrugged. "It's typical of MSBP."

Luke took a guess. "Was she making Alexia too sick to send to school? She's nearly five, isn't she?"

The ward supervisor looked surprised and impressed by Luke's quick-witted suggestion. "That fits the Munchausen's profile: possessive, wanting to look after the child for ever. Making her ill would be a way of doing it, I suppose."

"Any idea what killed her?"

She shook her head. "A heart attack. It'll be up to the pathologist to find out what brought it on. She was unconscious and dehydrated when she came in, and her blood pressure was sky-high."

Luke sighed and glanced at the door to the treatment room. "I'm still not intruding. Even if it's Wendy's fault — especially if it's her fault — she's going to be devastated. She needs some time alone."

"Almost alone," the ward supervisor replied.

Luke nodded. "Yes. Just a precaution. My mobile will record everything." He paused and then asked, "Could you make a note in your records of everyone who went in to try and save Alexia? While it's fresh in your mind."

"No problem. I'll do it now."

"Thanks. I'll wait for a bit before I disturb her mother."

"It's up to you, but I'm not sure it's the best time to question her."

"I'm not going to. Not now. I just need to check the

room out — and the body." Making sure that he was covering all angles, Luke added, "Can I use your computer? I want to request an agent to take Wendy home when she's ready."

"Another nice gesture?"

Luke smiled. "Not that nice. More a way of making sure a suspect doesn't run away."

It was tragic. Alexia Ridge was lying in a hospital bed and her feet reached only half way down its length. She was too thin for her height, probably a sign of ill health. Yet her long hair was beautifully groomed and arranged. Malc had told Luke that Wendy had spent a lot of time talking in private to her unhearing daughter and, at the same time, brushing her hair obsessively. Luke could not help recalling that his own mother had kept Kerryanne's hairbrush.

"The staff think Wendy made her ill because she's got Munchausen's Syndrome by Proxy. Did she say anything incriminating?"

Malc ran through his recording at maximum speed and then replied, "She did not make an unambiguous confession, but she said sorry nineteen times."

"Mmm. If Wendy made her ill," Luke said softly, "the question is, did her illness kill her or was that down to something that happened here? Compare the names of the staff who looked after Julian Bent with the ones who tried to revive Alexia. Does anyone crop up on both lists?"

A few seconds later, Malc answered, "There are no matching personnel."

Luke stopped at the end of the bed and shook his head at the sad sight of Alexia. "Can you take a blood sample?"

"Yes. However, the pathologist will complete a full post-mortem in due course."

"If her mother fed her something, I want to see if you can spot it straight away."

Malc manoeuvred himself over the small body. "Processing." He perched lightly on the girl's arm and directed a fine needle into the soft skin by her elbow. "Sample taken. Analysis in progress."

Luke walked round to the top of the bed. "There are tiny droplets on her forehead and neck."

"It is likely to be sweat, brought on by stress."

"Analyse that as well, please."

"Task logged. However, you should note that water will have been evaporating from the droplets for an unknown amount of time. Therefore, the concentration of substances will now be artificially high. Any such measurement will be unreliable and inadmissible."

"I want you to scan the whole room as well," said Luke, "and compare the results with what you found in Julian Bent's."

"I conducted a scan earlier, while the deceased's

mother was here. I will now compare the two sets of findings."

"Is there any sign of heather in here? I haven't seen any."

"Your observation is correct." Malc was silent for a minute and then announced, "There are no clear matches between traces detected in Julian Bent's room and those found in here. For example, there are no common hairs or fingerprints. Comparison of other biological samples — mainly flakes of skin — is not possible without DNA analysis."

"It might come to that."

"Performing DNA tests on all individual fragments would occupy my systems for a minimum of three continuous days."

"It's a job for the central lab, then."

Malc asked, "Do you wish me to request the resources?"

Luke nodded. "Mmm. Why not?"

"Because you have not yet established any crime, because the analysis will be very time-consuming, and because it will require an unwarranted number of technicians and instruments."

Suppressing a groan, Luke replied, "Put the request in anyway. It might turn something up — and it might help me to find out if there's a serial killer around here. That's worth the effort."

"Transmitting," Malc said. "I am continuing tests on Alexia Ridge's blood but I already have one significant result. It contains an excessive and lethal amount of sodium. Its concentration is nine point four times greater than the naturally occurring level."

"How could that have happened?" asked Luke.

"Sodium is essential for life and by far the main source is salt: sodium chloride. The kidneys regulate its concentration in the body. In healthy individuals, salt cannot rise naturally to such dangerous concentrations. It is ejected in sweat and urine. Therefore, poisoning is the probable cause."

"What's the effect of too much salt?"

"Hypernatremia causes dizziness, vomiting, diarrhoea and high blood pressure. Very high doses can trigger unconsciousness, stroke, heart attack and death."

"Are there any medical conditions that set it off?"

"There is a very rare disease called salt diabetes. It has never been reported in a child."

Luke took a breath and gazed down at Alexia. "So, she was poisoned with salt."

"Unproven but likely."

"What about these beads of sweat?"

"A person with hypernatremia would sweat profusely. These drops are very nearly saturated with sodium chloride. That is the result of evaporation, but excretion of salt is consistent with the proposed cause of death."

"Did Julian Bent show any sign of salt poisoning?"

"No."

"Was the salt level in his saline drip normal?"

"Yes."

Struck by a thought, Luke looked across at Malc. "You'd better find out if Wendy Ridge has got another child. If she has, the agent keeping her under surveillance needs to go in and check what's going on. If she's got Munchausen's, I don't want this to happen again."

After thirty seconds, Malc said, "The suspect has a three-year-old son."

"Well, if this is all about keeping her children instead of sending them to school, he's safe for a year. But if she just wants her kids to rely on her all the time, he's in danger."

"What is your recommendation to The Authorities?"

"Send the agent in. And check if she's making the boy sick with too much salt. If she is, he needs help – and so does she."

Chapter Eight

The office where Tara Fortune worked was not like a doctor's. In particular, there were no patients and no medical equipment. It was little more than a cupboard with a computer. When Luke held out his identity card towards her, Tara saved the data that she was handling, pushed aside a plate of biscuits and turned towards him with a quizzical expression. Barely older than Luke, she was very attractive with startlingly dark eyes. Her hair was so short that her head could have been shaved. "What can I do for you?" she asked with a wary smile.

There was nowhere for Luke to sit so he leaned against a wall. Pushing his long hair behind his ears, he said, "Do you like your job here?"

She frowned, probably unsure where Luke was going with his questioning. "Yeah, it's great. Kind of weird to be a mathematician when everyone else is into medicine and biology but. . ."

"When did you start?"

"Er. . . six months ago. Almost to the day." She began to fidget with her fingers as if she weren't used to doing nothing with them. Or maybe she was nervous.

"It's a strange set-up, isn't it? The Department of Alternative Medicine."

"I think it's good. More interesting than strange."

"You want it to be successful," Luke said.

"Of course, but. . . What are you getting at?"

"I suppose you calculate results, doing all the statistical stuff, finding out if a treatment's better than a placebo?"

It was a simple question but the answer came very slowly and deliberately. Tara was probably still trying to figure out if there was any harm in telling the truth. "Yes."

"Every time you get a positive result – showing some therapy really works – it's good for the department and keeps you in a job."

She didn't reply at once. After a moment's thought, she said, "It's even better for the patients."

Luke smiled and nodded. "Good point."

"As far as I can see, it's not about conventional versus alternative. It's about finding out what works and what doesn't. A lot of conventional therapies do wonders and some don't. Quite a few alternative medicines work as well, and some are rubbish. So what if we don't understand why? When I get ill, I just want something that works. I don't care if it's alternative or not understood, as long as it makes me better."

"Sounds sensible to me," said Luke. "Do you know Julian Bent?"

She didn't need to refer to her computer files. "Kind of. Acute pain case. Acupuncture treatment."

"I'm surprised you remember one patient so well."

Tara swallowed before replying. "He died. That's

61

terrible – and memorable. Anyway, it was only the day before yesterday."

"He didn't really have acupuncture, did he?"

"No. He was on the dummy needles."

"You remember that as well."

"Dr Sachs came in on Wednesday afternoon – to see his records."

Luke was careful to avoid reacting to his father's name. He interpreted Peter's reaction as perfectly innocent because he'd admitted that he kept an eye on the hospital's death statistics and checked out the fatalities.

"When you test a treatment, you do a double-blind experiment. Why do you keep the doctors and nurses in the dark? Why aren't they told who gets the remedy and who gets the placebo?"

"Two main reasons. If a nurse knows she's giving a dummy, patients can tell. They pick up little clues from her manner. That invalidates the trial. Everyone involved has got to behave the same way – thinking they're giving or getting the same thing. If they don't, you're kind of testing psychological effects, not the treatment. And when it comes to looking at the results, you don't want the doctor to be influenced by knowing who got what. You've got to be objective."

As a forensic investigator, Luke was supposed to be blind to bias as well. That's the way he'd been trained. But he couldn't be blind to the fact that Peter Sachs was his father. He was bound to be influenced. That's why he regarded Tara Fortune as a more serious suspect than his father.

"Did you ever visit Julian Bent?"

"No," she answered. "Patients are just names and numbers to me."

"So, you won't mind me taking a sample of your DNA to check."

Tara caught her breath but relented. "I've got nothing to hide."

Normally, he would opt for a hair with its root but Tara's hair was too short to tug out. Instead he took a cotton bud and rolled it against her inner cheek, then sealed it in a small evidence bag. "Thanks," he said. "That's about it. Except, do you keep a record of who carries out which test?"

"Yes. It's essential."

"Who gave Julian Bent his pretend-acupuncture?"

This time, Tara did have to resort to her computer. After a few seconds, she answered, "That was Dr Unwin and Nurse Young."

Luke learned nothing new from the Department of Alternative Medicine's acupuncture team of Nurse Young and Dr Unwin. They'd treated Julian Bent two days before his death and they hadn't noticed any flowers in his room. Neither of them had seen anything suspicious or heard of Alexia Ridge. And they'd both worked at the hospital for far longer than six months.

Luke took a couple of hairs from the doctor and the nurse – to identify any DNA that they'd left behind in Julian's room – and then went back to his hotel. He needed a break and a chat with Jade.

Appearing on Luke's telescreen, Jade said, "Hiya. Are you okay?"

"I'm flying, thanks," he replied, keeping quiet about his headache. "I saw my parents yesterday."

"You did what?" Jade exclaimed.

"My mother works just north of here and, in a way, my father's a suspect. Peter Sachs. He works at the hospital."

Jade hesitated and then laughed. "He must have loved seeing you! 'Here I am after eleven years. Your son. Now, answer these questions or I'm arresting you.' Fantastic."

Luke had to smile. "It didn't happen quite like that."

"What did you think of them?"

"Well, they know you're the Games' musician. They've seen you on telescreen. They said you looked nice."

"Yeah, but you're avoiding telling me what they're like," she replied.

"Mother's still grieving for Kerryanne – even after all this time. Father's almost as tall as me. Clever. And he drinks too much of something strange. He's grieving as well, I suppose."

"At least they've got each other."

"Yeah," Luke replied, "but I don't think it works like that. I got the feeling they don't get on very well. I reckon what happened to Kerryanne broke them up more than it pulled them together."

Jade nodded slowly. "Shame."

"Mother gave me some photos of her."

Jade cheered up. "Oh? What does she look like? Who does she look like?"

"I don't know," Luke confessed.

"Why not?"

He shrugged. "I can't look. Not yet. Today, I saw a little girl. . ."

"What? Dead?"

Luke nodded. "Probably poisoned by her mother. I couldn't look at photos of Kerryanne without thinking about her."

A look of horror came to Jade's face. "Are you saying your mother. . .?"

"No. Nothing like that. It was a brain tumour. That's all. It's just that. . . I suppose I don't want to see Kerryanne and feel guilty."

"Guilty?"

"Yes," Luke replied. "Guilty that she died and I didn't."

"You can't think like that."

"Mmm. Anyway," he said, steering her away from an uneasy topic, "they want to meet you."

"Me? Why?"

Luke shrugged again. "I don't know. They're interested in me, so I guess that makes them interested in you. Actually," he added, "it's strange. All through school, you get judged by results. Good marks and they like you. Bad marks and you're in trouble. But I got the impression my parents would like me for who I am, whether I did well or not."

"Unconditional support, eh?" Jade thought about it for a second and then grinned widely. "Weird, yes, but it sounds nice to me."

Luke gripped the sharp knife in his right hand and plunged it through the tough bronzed skin and into the soft flesh beneath. He lifted up the first quarter to his mouth and, avoiding the bitter membranes, sank his teeth into the red cells.

Watching the gruesome procedure, Malc said, "I have observed that you do not like to be interrupted during a pomegranate breakfast but you should know that you have been removed from the Wendy Ridge case."

Luke frowned, concerned that he didn't miss any of the seeds. "Oh?" he said. "Why?"

"Because it has been concluded overnight. When confronted with the evidence of excess salt in her daughter's body, Wendy Ridge confessed to making her ill but denied any intention to commit murder. She has been removed from her son to protect him."

"What'll happen to her now?"

"She will be tried on a nominal charge of malicious wounding. If found guilty, she will receive treatment rather than punishment."

"Sad but fair, I guess." Once Luke had finished breakfast, he pushed the wreckage of the pomegranate to one side and swallowed some painkillers. "Time for a shower. Do me a favour. If you receive any more messages while I'm in there, wait till I get out, eh?"

"I am expecting the first results from the analysis of traces in Julian Bent's hospital accommodation. If they are transmitted to me in the next few minutes, I will inform you after you come out of the bathroom."

"Tempting to stay in there all day," Luke mumbled to himself.

He couldn't avoid Malc for long. As soon as he came out of the shower, Malc started to recite the findings from Julian Bent's room. DNA fingerprinting had shown that Nurse Young and Dr Unwin had left fragments of skin behind. As Luke expected, there was no indication that Tara Fortune had been in the room. But the fourth result surprised and horrified him.

Malc announced, "A faint DNA trace matched perfectly against the hospital records for Dr Peter Sachs."

"What?"

"A faint DNA trace matched—"

"But. . ." On edge, Luke folded his arms tightly across

his stomach. "It can't be!"

"The chances of an accidental match are——"

"Yes, I know," Luke snapped. "It's unheard of."

"Your presence is requested at the hospital," said Malc.

Luke did not respond. He was still thinking about his father.

Malc repeated, "Your presence is requested——"

"What is it?" Luke muttered.

"Another death has occurred."

Chapter Nine

Outside the hotel, the air was rich with the characteristic sweet smell from the chocolate factory. As Luke walked away, his hair still wet, he asked Malc to provide a sound-only link to Peter Sachs. When Malc made the connection, the doctor was in a cab making for the hospital from the opposite direction. Hesitantly, Luke said, "You. . . er. . . you told me Julian Bent's name sounded familiar but you couldn't remember him being your department's patient. But Tara Fortune said you checked his file out on Wednesday afternoon."

Malc relayed Dr Sachs's voice. "Sorry, Luke. It slipped my mind. Elisa's always going on about how forgetful I am these days. Must have been the excitement of seeing you."

"Did you ever go to his room?"

"No."

"Sure?" Luke checked.

"Absolutely certain."

Luke could not cope with any more questions right now. "Okay," he said. "Thanks. I'll be in touch."

"Excellent." His father sounded pleased.

Luke felt the opposite.

When he reached the hospital, he made directly for the orthopaedics section where a middle-aged man called

Charlie Illingworth had died one and a half hours previously. Luke had never seen anything like it. The body in the bed was not limp. He was as rigid as a stone statue. His arms were folded across his chest and his hands were clenched tightly into fists. His head was not resting on the pillow. It poked up unnaturally, locked into position by a totally stiff neck.

"I don't know why you're getting involved," the doctor said. "There's an obvious cause of death. He had fibrodysplasia ossificans progressiva – or FOP for short. It's rare but it turns muscle, tendons and ligaments into bone. Inside him, there's a second skeleton that should be muscle. That's why he's rigid. The staff call it stone-man syndrome for obvious reasons."

"That's terrible," Luke said, pulling a face. "Couldn't you do anything for him?"

"There's no treatment, no cure. We just tried to make him comfortable."

"Did the Department of Alternative Medicine have anything to do with him?"

"No."

"Not even as a control?"

"No."

Luke almost breathed a sigh of relief. His father did not have a motive for murder because Charlie Illingworth's death could not improve his department's results. Luke looked around the room. "I'll tell you why

70

I'm getting involved." He pointed to the clutter on the bedside table. "That."

The doctor looked amazed. "Flowers?"

"Check it, Malc. Is it the same heather as the bit in Julian Bent's room?"

"Confirmed."

Talking to the doctor again, Luke asked, "Do you know who gave him the bunch of heather?"

"That'll be the Heather Man."

"The Heather Man? Who's he?"

"Oh, he's harmless. Been handing it round for years. No one knows who he is, but some say he was a patient here once." She shrugged.

"Have you seen him?"

"Not personally, no. But everyone knows about him. A bit of a legend."

"Why does he do it?"

She shrugged. "It's supposed to be lucky, isn't it? Maybe he's just kind, trying to cheer people up who haven't got much to be cheerful about," she said, glancing down at the human statue.

"If you – or any of the staff – see him, let me know."

"Not much chance of that. As I understand it, he doesn't exactly keep a schedule. He just appears now and again." The doctor hesitated and then said, "It's pretty obvious what killed Mr Illingworth. So, will you release his body? Sorry, but the Institute of Biomechanical

Research is eager to get their hands on him before decomposition sets in. They don't often get the chance to study an unusual specimen like this."

"Have they got permission already?"

"From me, yes. He hasn't got a partner so there's no one else." She shrugged. "It's sad but who would you pair him with? A normal life's out of the question. He was born with a death sentence and he's been edging towards it ever since, getting progressively worse."

"Are any of his organs up for transplant?"

The doctor grimaced. "No chance. Look at him. No one would want the heart of a stone man."

Luke nodded. "All right. Give me a few minutes to scan around, then you can take the body away. But I don't want anyone else in here till a team of agents comes to collect forensic samples."

"Well, I think you're wasting your time, but it's up to you."

Left alone in Charlie Illingworth's room, Luke said, "Take a full scan, Malc, but there's something I want you to look for in particular."

"Specify."

Luke sighed. "My father's DNA."

"Processing."

Watching his mobile float across the room from side to side, Luke asked, "Has Julian Bent's body gone to this Institute of Biomechanical Research?"

"No."

"But have they used more bodies than normal in the past six months?"

Already engaged in scanning and sampling for DNA, Malc took nearly three minutes to consult hospital records. "They have taken possession of a slightly greater proportion of corpses than they did in the same period last year. It does not amount to an increase of twenty to thirty bodies."

"So, it's out of step with the number of extra deaths. Even so," Luke replied, "it's time I paid them a visit."

While Malc completed his tasks, Luke was transfixed by the sculpture of Charlie Illingworth. The man's unusual disease had turned him into a wasted figure before it had finally brought him to a permanent halt, like a robot with an exhausted battery.

"I have collected sufficient samples," Malc announced. "A rapid assessment of the DNA present will occupy my analytical resources for three to three and a half hours. Full DNA analysis of any traces that may have come from Dr Sachs will take further time."

"All right. Get on with it. But have you detected any biscuit crumbs?"

"No."

"Okay. I'm going to take a look at the Institute of Biomechanical Research."

The Institute's laboratories were cooled to prevent

rapid decomposition of the specimens. Malc could have measured the low temperature precisely with his digital thermometer. But the atmosphere was also cold in a way that Malc could not calculate. It was the chill of the department's unsettling work.

Oscar Hislop was wearing two jumpers underneath his lab coat. "This is a liver," he said, slapping a squishy organ down on the bench as if he were an attendant serving Luke with a dish of raw meat. "If I press it hard but slowly with my hand, the water inside moves out of the way. The liver flattens out and comes back to shape when I take my hand away. It's bouncy like a ball. But if I apply the same pressure suddenly with a hammer – something that might happen if someone got hit by a fast cab – it shatters. That's because the internal water doesn't get the time to move away from the blow. Not good news if the liver's inside you at the time. And it's even worse after a meal because the liver stiffens up a bit then." Clearly enthusiastic about his work and fond of shocking visitors, the biomechanical engineer grinned. "It's an organ that bounces or splats depending on how you apply the force."

Luke shivered. Behind him, there was a loud bang that made him jump. "What was that?" he exclaimed.

Unperturbed, Oscar said, "One of my colleagues is in the cold room – really cold, not like in here – with a fresh corpse. He's firing some new types of bullet into its head and heart, studying what happens."

Luke did not reply but he screwed up his face in disgust. The place seemed to be a twisted cross between an abattoir and a testing station.

Oscar made a tutting noise with his tongue. "Where do you think your mobile aid to law and crime gets all its data about damage to human bodies? Someone's got to do it. And we've been doing it for ages, hidden away down here in the basement, out of the public gaze. The institute's very first experiment, eighty years ago, got a load of dead bodies and dropped them head-first from different heights onto a concrete floor to see how big an impact fractures skulls. Most people would rather not know about it. They might like to think it doesn't happen, but it does. And we're all a lot better off for the knowledge. The thing that came out of that first research was a properly designed helmet to protect the head from impacts."

On the opposite wall, there was a giant telescreen split into a three-by-three grid showing nine ongoing medical operations. Viewing the complex display, one of Oscar's colleagues tapped at a keypad to bring one particular operation to full screen. Seeing a scalpel delving into a brain, Luke was grateful that his vision was still not perfect.

He swallowed and turned back to Oscar. "I guess there's no shortage of bodies when you're attached to the hospital."

"Supply's not normally a problem. Partners often give permission." He shrugged and smiled. "The dead haven't got any use for their bodies, have they? And neither have the living. Apart from us, that is. Having them cremated is a waste of a valuable resource. Better to use them for scientific study."

This time, Luke didn't jolt so much when the gun fired for a second time in the adjoining laboratory. "So, you don't have to go into the rest of the hospital, touting for business?"

Oscar laughed. "It's a nice image. 'We'll have her over there when she dies because we need lungs like hers. Good muscles on the next one so we'll have him as well.' No. That'd be. . . disrespectful, wouldn't it? We put a call out through the hospital computer for the sort of thing we want. Then, a ward supervisor will tell us when they've got something interesting if the partner's likely to agree. All very discreet and simple."

Despite Oscar's reply, Luke wondered if he or one of his colleagues roamed the wards looking out for people with particular appeal, like patients suffering from fibrodysplasia ossificans progressiva. It would be a short step between earmarking them for use after death and hastening their availability. Luke asked, "Did you know about Charlie Illingworth?"

"Who?"

"A patient who's just died with stone-man syndrome."

"Ah, yes. We avoid using names. That makes things too personal. To us, he'll be reduced to initials. Yes, I knew we'd got a stone man coming in. Very rare. We're very excited."

Luke nodded. "I guess Charlie isn't so excited."

"Charlie – CI – won't know much about it," Oscar replied.

"Correction," Malc added. "The subject will not know anything about it."

Chapter Ten

Sheathed in glass, the three futuristic towers of York School glinted in the sunshine. In a common room on the second floor of the accommodation block, Luke waited by the window and watched the large wheel rotating leisurely down by the river. He turned towards Mr Peacock and said, "The school's a surprise. It specializes in history but it's really modern."

"Life's full of contradictions," he replied frostily.

The instructor's gruff response made Luke grateful that he'd come to interview someone else. He was hoping to learn about the Heather Man from a familiar and friendly face.

When Nyree Max dashed in, she was wearing a big grin. "Sorry, I was out playing. . ." She gazed at Luke and said, "Are you all right now?"

Luke smiled at her. Unwilling to disappoint her with the truth about his aches and pains, he answered, "I'm fine, thanks."

Out of breath, Nyree flopped into a seat. "When they told me you wanted to see me, I ran. Anyway, I'm here now."

"You must be fit and well again."

She nodded. "The only thing is, the school doesn't spoil me any more."

"There's a black cloud to every silver lining," said Luke.

Nyree giggled. It wasn't a great joke but she looked ready to jump at any chance to laugh.

"Have you still got your pyramid?"

Nyree shook her head. "Had to take it back."

Luke didn't quiz her about it. He wasn't really interested in her lucky charm. He mentioned it only to put the ten-year-old at ease and to keep her chatting. "I want to ask you about your stay in hospital," he said.

Luke didn't need Nyree's tutor to be present, but Mr Peacock had insisted. The instructor watched the proceedings in sinister silence.

"Oh? Why?" Nyree asked.

"It's a nuisance, but someone's worried about procedures and stuff. Very boring. I've been given the job of looking into it, I'm afraid. I just wondered if you'd come across someone called the Heather Man."

Nyree nodded enthusiastically. "He's nice. Kind. He goes around giving people heather for good luck. I didn't see him this time, but he gave me a bunch last time I had to go in for a couple of days."

"What's his name? Do you know?"

She shook her head. "Didn't say."

Luke looked at Mr Peacock. "Have you seen him? Do you know who he is?"

"No."

79

Luke turned back to Nyree. "Can you describe him? His age, hair, height, anything."

Nyree gazed at the ceiling for a few seconds, as if seeking inspiration. "He was old. I don't know, but over forty, I suppose. He was a lot shorter than you. About the same as Mr Peacock. He didn't have a beard, but he was all sort of rough." She ran her hand over her cheeks and chin to show Luke where the Heather Man had stubble. "His hair was dark but quite a lot was going grey."

"What was he wearing?"

Nyree took a deep breath. "I can't remember. Sorry. He isn't in trouble, is he?"

"I don't know till I catch up with him. Hopefully not. What about his voice?"

"He spoke quiet."

At once, Mr Peacock corrected her. "Quietly."

"Yes," Nyree said. "Quietly, like he was feeling weak."

"Did he tell you anything about himself?"

"No," Nyree answered. "He was far more interested in me. Asked me if I was in pain and that sort of thing. Oh, he did say. . ."

"What?"

"Nothing really. He told me where he got the heather from. A healer who lives in a cabin down by the Ouse. The Heather Man said this old guy had things that'd fix people when normal medicine didn't work. You know. So, I went." She glanced across at Mr Peacock. "That's where

I got the jade pyramid from. Jade gives you good health."

Luke changed his mind. He was much more interested in the pyramid now, but he still didn't believe in its healing powers. "When you were in hospital, what treatment did you get – apart from the pyramid?"

"New tablets, and they did this funny thing with my head. They strapped two damp sponges to it and passed some electricity—"

Mr Peacock interrupted. "It's called transcranial direct current stimulation."

"Yes," Nyree agreed, her offhand tone revealing that she didn't care what the procedure was called. "It doesn't hurt. Just a tingle. It's a tiny current, but it's supposed to make migraines better. They say it makes you brainier and helps you get your memory back, if you've lost it."

It sounded like a cure that Luke's father might try. And it might have been successful. While Nyree put her recovery down to the jade pyramid, Luke believed much more in a new drug or an alternative treatment that actually did something. "I might have to go and see this old healer."

Looking worried, Nyree asked, "Are you still sick?"

Luke thought of his headaches and his still fuzzy vision but he denied it. "No. It's just that he might be able to point me in the direction of the Heather Man."

"Well, you can't miss the shack. That's what the Heather Man said. It's got heather all round it."

The riverside quarter of York was easily within walking distance but Luke didn't reach it. Reporting on the DNA discovered in Charlie Illingworth's room, his mobile stopped him in his tracks. "Subject to confirmation by a full analysis," Malc said, "I have found a fragment containing Dr Peter Sachs's genetic material."

Stunned, Luke stared at his mobile. "But the doctor said the alternative medicine people didn't have anything to do with Charlie Illingworth."

"Correct. Therefore, this finding is suspicious."

Luke put his head in his hands for a moment. When he looked up again, he said, "All right. Back to the hospital. Let's get it over with."

The chief consultant of the Department of Alternative Medicine was taking a lunch break – and a drink – in his office when Luke entered. Peter put the glass down and beamed at his son. "Not a murmur for eleven years, and now you can't keep away from me!" he laughed.

"Sorry," said Luke, "but something's cropped up. I've got to ask if you're treating a patient called Charlie Illingworth."

Peter frowned and thought about it for a second. "No. I don't think so. Which ward is he in?"

Luke was pleased to note that his father had not used the past tense. He didn't seem to know that Charlie was dead. "Orthopaedics. He's not a patient you'd forget in a hurry."

"Oh? Why's that?"

"He's got – I mean, he had – stone-man syndrome."

"That's the one where muscles convert to bone."

"Yes," Luke replied.

Peter shook his head. "No, we've never taken that on. It's very rare. And unimaginably nasty."

"So, you'd remember if you'd visited him?"

Peter nodded. "Certainly would. It'd be like seeing a disaster you can't do anything about. You'd never forget standing beside a volcano when it erupted. Stone-man syndrome's like that. A slow eruption inside the body."

Luke steeled himself, looked towards Malc and said, "Do we have DNA evidence that Dr Peter Sachs was in the rooms where Julian Bent and Charlie Illingworth were patients?"

Malc answered, "Confirmed."

Peter appeared to be shocked for an instant. Then he put up both hands, as if in defence. "I can assure you, Luke, I haven't been in either."

Luke was struggling to explain the result unless. . . He gazed at his father and asked, "Do you happen to have an identical twin?"

"Clever question. But no. You've got an aunt. She's a few years older than me. That's all."

"So, how do you explain. . .?"

Dismissing the DNA evidence, Peter shrugged. "I don't. I can't. But right now, something else is worrying me more."

"What's that?"

"Are you feeling all right? You look washed out."

"I'm fine." Actually, Luke was fretting that he would have to arrest his own father if he came across any more incriminating data.

Peter's face was contorted with concern. "When you're sixteen, you think you're indestructible. Let me tell you, you're not. I work in a hospital. I've seen it too many times, Luke. Get yourself checked out."

"Okay, but one more thing. Do you do transcranial direct current stimulation?"

"Yes. It's simple – barely more than a battery and a couple of wires – but it really helps some people."

"Do you remember Nyree Max?"

Peter let out a sigh. "Young girls tend to stay in my mind. Ever since Kerryanne. . . you understand."

"Was she getting the real thing or a placebo?"

"I don't know. I'd have to ask Tara."

Luke shrugged. "Never mind."

The joy of seeing Luke again drained from Peter's face. Suddenly, he looked tired and drawn. "She hasn't died as well, has she?"

"No," Luke answered. "You can put her down as a success."

Relieved, Peter closed his eyes for a couple of seconds. When he opened them, he said, "Thank goodness for that."

To Luke, he seemed too considerate to be capable of taking life away.

His long legs dangling over the quayside, Luke's shoes were just a few centimetres above the surging river. Winter sunshine glinted on the surface of the water, burned Luke's eyes, and coloured his vision. To his left, the decorative stone bridge carried electric cabs across the Ouse. A gauge was attached to the middle arch of the bridge, showing the height of the water above normal levels. Actually, it was more than an indication of imminent flooding. It was part of an automated flood-avoidance system. When the gauge reached a critical level – as it did last November when the rains finally came in great bursts – a signal went upstream and opened gates to divert the excess into flood plains.

Luke was occupied more with Peter Sachs. "No," he insisted, "he can't be a murderer. Not my own father. Not a doctor."

Always completely objective, Malc replied, "Illogical and incorrect. You are being influenced by your own body chemistry. When a human being forms a bond with another person, the body makes hormones called oxytocin and vasopressin. These act on the amygdala in the brain, switching off the mechanism that initiates feelings of distrust and fear. In the absence of these

85

feelings, negative judgements and suspicion do not arise, making it possible to form a trusting and unconditional relationship. Therefore, the individual concerned always appears trustworthy and perfect. This is the biochemical basis for the proverb, 'Love is blind'. It explains your attitude to Jade Vernon and it is also the reason you refuse to accept that your father is the chief suspect."

Luke eyed his mobile. "That's it, is it? It's all down to hormones floating around my brain?"

"Confirmed."

"If my father murdered the stone man somehow, why did he do it?"

"Insufficient data. The fact that a suspect's motive is unknown at this time does not eliminate him from the investigation."

Luke knew better than to argue with Malc. He had as much chance of changing the mobile's verdict as he had of stopping the river flowing by jumping in and ordering the water to turn back. He got to his feet again and said, "Come on. I want to find the healer's cabin."

Chapter Eleven

Going along the picturesque riverside walkway, Luke said, "I don't really know why I'm chasing the Heather Man so much. Because he went into two rooms where patients died, I suppose. But no one's got a bad word for him. All he seems to do is cheer people up."

"He could be a witness and he remains a suspect," Malc replied factually.

Luke came to a halt beside a rock garden of heathers that encircled an untidy wooden trailer in this pretty part of York. "Here we are," he said. The cabin's paintwork had once been gaudy but now it was faded and peeling. Even so, displays of cute trinkets brightened the drab windows.

"The flowerbeds contain *Erica carnea*," Malc informed him.

"Okay, thanks." Luke opened the door cautiously but, for security, Malc entered first. The fragrance of herbs and spices drifted over them both. Scented candles lit the shed, revealing an old man sitting on the other side of a counter-cum-workbench. When the door closed behind Luke, it seemed to cut him off from the rest of York.

The artist, rumoured to be a healer, raised his face towards his visitors. He cast a cursory glance at Malc but he gazed intently at Luke. His expression suggested a mixture of curiosity and compassion.

Luke nodded at him. Before he asked any questions, though, Luke decided to look around. On the right-hand shelving, he hesitated by a handwritten label that read, "Items in hard jade bring the owner good health". Thinking of Nyree, Luke smiled wryly. Almost at once, a lush green pyramid caught his eye. As far as he could remember, it was exactly the same as the one he'd seen in Nyree's hands when she'd been discharged from hospital. Solid and slick in dark green. Maybe it was the same one. He reached out and clasped it in both hands.

Crawford Gallagher watched the forensic investigator closely. Hobbling slowly, he made his way down the aisle towards Luke.

When Luke stopped gazing at the shiny pyramid and looked at the healer he felt uncomfortable, because the old man was staring uncannily at the exact spot on his head that was throbbing relentlessly.

On edge, Luke said, "Er. . . just being nosy."

The man's intense expression changed. He glanced down at the pyramid and then winked at Luke. "That's very special. I can see why it's chosen you."

Luke frowned. "You mean, why I chose it."

"I meant what I said." Strangely, the healer lifted his hand towards the sore area above Luke's left ear but, when Malc moved in protectively, he withdrew it. "The pyramid will make a difference. This is what you do. You take it home, yes? You touch one of the green sides against here." His wrinkled hand went to his own head, touching the same spot that was plaguing Luke. "Then you put it by your bed and sleep with a lamp on so its shadow falls on you all night."

"And what does that do?" asked Luke.

"That heals."

There was something about the old man's sincerity and confidence that Luke did not want to dent. He decided not to deny the pyramid's power. "I don't need. . . I mean, that's not why I came. It's. . . er. . . interesting but not. . ." He began to replace the ornament on the display.

Crawford touched his arm to stop him. "No. Believe me. You keep it. It's yours. No one must disturb you during pyramid time. Afterwards, you return it to me. Understand? It does not work again, you see. Like a toy with batteries, it runs down after a cure. It's yours to use and then you bring it back for me to recharge the batteries."

Luke decided it was time to get official. Holding the pyramid in one hand, he showed his identity card with the other. "Luke Harding, forensic investigator."

The man shook his head and waved away the plastic identity card with his knobbly hand. "I don't need a name. Just use the pyramid well. But only once and never again. Twice is very dangerous."

Luke decided that it was easier just to accept the healer's offering. Then perhaps he could get the man to talk about something else. "All right. Thanks. But I'm afraid *I* do need names. What's yours?"

"Pah," the artist said, turning away dismissively. Even so, he answered Luke's question. "Crawford Gallagher."

Following Crawford back towards the counter, Luke said, "I came to trace a man – maybe forty, maybe older – who takes heather from you."

"No, you didn't. Maybe you think you did."

"How do you mean?"

Crawford leaned on the workbench's wooden surface, littered with half-finished figurines and sprigs of heather. "You came for a cure. Whether you know it or not, that's what drove you here."

Luke nodded. "But, while I'm here, I'm trying to find out about the Heather Man. That's what they call him at the hospital."

Crawford did not seem interested. He looked out of a window instead.

"He's quietly spoken. A lot shorter than me, quite a bit of stubble, dark but greying hair."

Crawford sighed. Reluctantly, he said, "Yes, I know him."

"What's his name?"

"I don't need names," he repeated.

Luke tried a different angle. "Does he come here a lot?"

"Huh. From time to time. Often, he just helps himself

from my garden and goes. He thinks I don't see. But I know he's taking it out of pity for others."

"So, you've spoken to him."

"Not really. I just know."

"You also seem to know about illnesses," Luke said. "Is the Heather Man poorly?"

"Not now, but he has the look about him. He's been right up to the door."

"Pardon?"

"He's been to death's door. Something brought him back."

Luke nodded again. He did not believe that he was going to get any further with Crawford Gallagher so he said, "Thanks. I'll leave you in peace."

When Luke and Malc walked away, Crawford stood at the window and watched them leave with a wistful expression on his withered face.

Back in the bright light, Luke's eyes stung and watered immediately. Through the drumming in his skull, he mumbled, "Weird."

"It is not illegal to be weird," Malc replied.

"Just as well," Luke muttered. He held the pyramid under one arm and took the tube of painkillers out of his pocket with his other hand. He flicked the container open and swallowed two tablets. Grasping the jade ornament in both hands again, he raised it a little and said, "I'm going to dump this back at the hotel before I get on."

Luke stood to one side as two hospital porters and a doctor flew down the corridor with a trolley case. A monitor mounted on the side of the trolley was recording the unlucky patient's vital functions and emitting bleeps. For a moment, Luke watched the dash and thought about the end of his last inquiry when he'd been the emergency. He'd been rushed from London to York in a frantic bid to be treated at a specialist unit. It was all a great contrast with Crawford Gallagher's quiet, mystical and probably useless version of healing.

Emphasizing that Luke was back in the normal high-tech world, Malc announced, "I have received DNA profiles from the room where Alexia Ridge died. There are no matches with those found near Julian Bent and Charlie Illingworth."

"So, no trace of Peter Sachs?"

"Confirmed."

"That makes sense. I don't think Alexia Ridge has got anything to do with my case. The other two might not either, but I've got to assume they have for now. Anyway, Alexia's the odd one out. She didn't have a disease. The men were both seriously ill. Charlie was terminally ill."

"In addition," Malc said, "Julian Bent and Charlie Illingworth both had heather in their rooms and Dr Sachs visited them at least once each."

"Mmm. So did the Heather Man – probably. But. . ."

Luke shrugged helplessly. "Father denies it and the Heather Man's not around to ask."

That was why Luke was strolling around the wards of York Hospital, looking for patients with heather and talking to ward supervisors.

He had his first success in the next section. The supervisor scratched his head. "Heather? Yes. Last week, we sent a woman home. Sandy Chipperfield. She had a sprig of the stuff with her. Not very showy, is it? Anyway, I remember because it fell off her wheelchair and I picked it up for her."

"When you say you sent her home, do you mean she got better?"

"No," the ward supervisor answered. "I mean the opposite. We couldn't do any more for her, sadly. She was in the final stages of motor neurone disease. She's had a quiet private death at home, the way it should be."

"Would anyone ask the pathologist to check out a death like that?" asked Luke.

"What's the point? Doing a post-mortem would just tell us what we already know. Motor neurone disease kills people." He shrugged. "I imagine a busy pathologist has got better things to do."

"Have you seen the Heather Man at all?"

"No. But I'm glad he does what he does. It's kind."

"Yes. Thanks," Luke said.

Luke regarded his investigation as bizarre. He had

some suspects for a crime, but he didn't have a cause of death or a motive. He didn't even have clear victims. Or a clear crime. He wasn't going to give up, though. He was determined to understand why there were too many deaths at the hospital. He just had to hope that the reason was nothing to do with Dr Peter Sachs. But Luke still didn't know why his father was lying about visiting patients.

Luke examined the directions displayed on the wall outside the ward and then headed further along the wide passageway. "Let's try the Phobia Clinic down here," he said to his mobile.

When the door to the clinic slid aside, Luke and Malc entered the reception area where six people were waiting. One of them – an unkempt middle-aged man – took one look at the forensic investigator and his mobile, stood up, and made a run for it. In a second, he'd disappeared through the exit on the opposite side of the reception.

Luke groaned. He didn't really feel up to a chase, but he burst into a run anyway.

Chapter Twelve

Luke dodged around the rows of seats and dashed out of the same exit. Behind him, the Phobia Clinic's receptionist shouted something but the door closed, cutting him off. Besides, Luke was more intent on catching the jumpy patient who matched Nyree's description of the Heather Man.

Finding himself in a short empty passageway, Luke sprinted to the end. There, to the right, was an open hallway with a fire exit and three elevators. The shiny metallic door of one of the elevators slid shut before Luke could see who was inside, but he guessed that the man who'd been in the waiting area was getting away from him. The digital display above the elevator told him that the contraption was going up. The other two elevators were both halted on lower floors.

Making a decision, Luke shouted, "This way!" He barged through the door to the stairs. He dashed up the first flight of the fire exit, two steps at a time, before coming to an abrupt halt. Listening intently, he said, "What's that noise?"

"Below you, a person is going down," Malc replied. "The footsteps indicate a hurried descent."

Luke hesitated only for a fraction of a second. "Right. The elevator was a decoy. Come on!" He turned round and went down the steps as fast as he could without falling.

Malc couldn't take a short cut by plunging straight down the stairwell because it wasn't wide enough to take his bulk. Instead, Luke said, "Go on ahead. Defence mode. Stop him."

The mobile went in front but could not accelerate to his maximum speed because the stairs zigzagged and he had to slow down to take the corners. Even so, Malc was quicker than a human being.

Confident in his Mobile Aid to Law and Crime, Luke eased up on his breakneck speed. In a few seconds, Malc was out of view, closing in on the man with the stubbly neck and chin. Luke sighed and steadied himself with a hand on the rail. Only two or three storeys to go before he reached the ground floor.

Then, further down the stairwell, there was the sound of a door slamming and a loud thump. Alert and curious, Luke quickened his pace again.

From the top of the final flight, Luke saw Malc leaning against the fire door, unable to get through. Descending the last few steps, he called, "What happened?"

"The suspect reached the door first. He has pushed something against the exterior to deny my passage. It is against the law to obstruct—"

"Stand back."

Luke rushed at the door and hit it with his right foot.

He hoped that it would swing fully open but it moved only a few centimetres. Using his leg, he pushed with all his strength, forcing it open until the gap was wide enough for himself and Malc. Outside, he barely glanced at the large rubbish bin that had been shoved hurriedly up against it. On his toes, Luke looked both ways, trying to pick out the fleeing patient. Most of the people in view were going to the right, heading for the city centre. Many of them were probably coming away from sporting events. To the left, the walkway went towards the Ouse. He saw no sign of the man he wanted to question.

Luke was tall but he was no match for Malc who rose up above the ground and then announced, "The suspect is going in the direction of the river."

At once, Luke ran down the busy walkway, brushing against a couple emerging from one of the restaurants. He squeezed sideways between a walkway lamp and a group of visitors outside a souvenir stall. Weaving around the pedestrians in his path, he hurried towards the bridge where the walkway converged with a corridor to make a crossing over the river for both pedestrians and cabs. Going past the grand entrance to York Museum, where four girls were singing a rude song about their football team's opponents, Luke gasped, "Have you still got him under surveillance, Malc?"

"No. My systems have lost track of him."

"Great!"

"Your remark is in blatant conflict with expectation. I deduce that you are using irony."

Keeping going, Luke muttered, "Good deduction."

With Malc hovering at his shoulder, Luke dashed onto the bridge, slowed down and came to a halt. He didn't see any sense in continuing a chase when he had no idea where his target had gone. With hands on hips and heaving shoulders, he took some deep breaths. "I'm nowhere near fit yet."

Directly below Luke, a river launch pulled out from the jetty and sped north. At its prow was the man with something to hide. He hadn't run onto the bridge. He'd taken the slipway down to the river and escaped on a boat.

Luke leaned on the handrail and groaned. He could do nothing but watch the patient getting away.

Incapable of feeling disappointment, Malc said, "I will be able to identify him by chemical analysis of the traces left on the door of the fire exit and by analysing his fingerprints on the rubbish bin that he moved."

Still getting his breath back, Luke found something to smile about. "Okay. We'll have a competition. You do that and I'll go back to the Phobia Clinic and ask who he was."

After two and a half seconds, Malc replied, "Your method has merit. It will almost certainly provide a quicker result."

"So, you're throwing in the towel?"

Clearly unable to figure out the meaning of Luke's words, Malc said, "I do not possess a towel."

"Oh well. Never mind. Let's go back to the hospital."

The receptionist at the clinic shook his head irritably.

"Didn't you hear me? I did try to tell you."

"Tell me what?" Luke asked.

"I shouted. Mr Wilkins has technophobia, a fear of advanced machines. Your Mobile Aid to Law and Crime will have sent him into a panic. The worst thing you could've done is chase him with a robot."

"Ah."

"Exactly," the receptionist replied angrily. "I don't know how much you've set him back."

"Sorry, but. . ." Luke decided not to defend himself. There wasn't much point. He couldn't undo what he'd done. "Is he the Heather Man, do you know?"

"Who's the Heather Man?"

"Haven't you heard of him?"

"No," the receptionist answered. "I haven't been here long."

"Have you ever seen Mr Wilkins with bunches of heather?"

"No. Never."

"All right," said Luke. "Thanks. And sorry again."

The receptionist typed something into his computer. "I guess we'll just have to repair the damage, if he finds

99

the courage to come back and continue his treatment."

"How long's he been a patient?"

Glancing at the computer screen, the receptionist replied, "Six months."

Chapter Thirteen

Outside the Phobia Clinic, Luke threw up his arms.

"Now what?"

Almost at once, he got an answer to his question. Further down the passageway, a door opened and the biomechanical engineer, Oscar Hislop, emerged. Without a glance towards Luke, he slipped away from the ward in the other direction.

Luke's curiosity kicked in immediately. "What's he doing up here? Come on. I want to find out." Luke strode down the corridor towards the Brain Injury Unit.

The ward was quiet. It was Saturday evening and the consultants had finished their rounds. Only emergency doctors remained on duty. There was another reason for the calm. Laid out in a sad row, the patients were eerily inactive. They had disorders such as brain tumours, Alzheimer's disease, and variant CJD. If Kerryanne were alive, this is where she would have been nursed. In a queue, going nowhere.

Luke held out his identity card for the supervisor. "You've just had a visit from Oscar Hislop," he said in a hushed voice.

The ward supervisor shuddered. "Creepy man. Well intentioned, of course, but I still think his line of work is sinister."

"What was he after?"

"Nothing, really. He was just asking about my patients."

"He must've had a reason."

"Well, yes. It sounds bad – morbid really – but he's got to be prepared, I suppose. He's planning some experiments on diseased brains and he needs slices of tissue to work with."

Keeping to a respectful whisper, Luke said, "So, he was wondering if you've got any patients whose brains are going to become available soon."

The supervisor nodded.

Luke asked, "And do you?"

The ward supervisor sighed. She waved her hand towards the row of spent patients. "Take your pick."

Despite what Hislop had said under questioning, he did trawl the wards for human bodies and tissue. "The thing is, did Oscar Hislop take his pick?"

"He's not that creepy. He just wanted access to our medical files so he could see which patients would suit him best. I don't think he'll have long to wait in some cases."

"Did he touch any patients or equipment while he was here?"

"No."

"Did you leave him alone at any point?"

"I don't really think—"

Luke interrupted. "Did you?"

"Only for a few seconds. A nurse called me away for a bit."

Luke nodded. "All right. Just let me know straight away if anything happens." He turned to go but then hesitated. "Have you – or any of your patients – seen the Heather Man?"

The ward supervisor smiled. "Does he really exist? Isn't he just a myth? I don't know, but he hasn't been in here. We're a heather-free zone."

Usually, Luke was working in the south and there would be little to do at night but continue his criminal investigation. He would use the evenings to sift through notes or mull over the results of forensic tests. While he was doing it, he would gaze at artificial stars or listen to downloads of Jade's music. Now he was in York, there were lots of things to do on a Saturday night. The place was alive with different forms of entertainment. Luke could even take a cab and meet Jade at one of her Sheffield gigs. Even though he had plenty of options, he didn't really feel like taking advantage of the distractions. He was tired and tender.

He was sure that his headache would go away once he'd had more time to recover from the injuries he'd suffered in his last case. He didn't want to panic everyone by asking for a brain scan when it was probably just a hangover from a tangle with the saboteur he'd called

Spoilsport.

He lay back on the bed, closed his eyes, and fell asleep almost at once.

An hour later, Malc received a communication. "We will talk to Forensic Investigator Luke Harding for an update on the York Hospital case." The code linked to the message told Malc that it had come from The Authorities.

Malc's speech circuitry composed his reply. He transmitted it in silence because it was pointless to express it aloud. "FI Harding is asleep."

"You will wake him."

Still in mute mode, Malc sent his response. "I will not comply."

Shaken by the mobile's disobedience, the voice of The Authorities was silent for a moment. "You will wake him," she repeated in a slow clear voice, apparently convinced that the mobile must have misheard her the first time.

"I am programmed to protect FI Harding and oversee his recuperation. I estimate that he requires rest to return to health."

"Are you saying he's still ill?"

"His life signs are weaker than usual but within normal range."

"Continue monitoring. Call for a doctor if his condition becomes unstable."

"Your command is unnecessary because I am already programmed to do so."

"Perhaps you'd better update me on the investigation."

"I will prepare a summary and transmit it to you."

"Good. In the meantime, we need to know if FI Harding has worked out why York Hospital is experiencing a significant number of extra deaths."

"He has several lines of inquiry but insufficient data to progress beyond speculation. There is no obvious evidence of murder."

"We expect progress," the voice retorted. "We can't have a major hospital's reputation tainted for longer than absolutely necessary."

At some point in the night, Luke stirred. Maybe he was dreaming, maybe he was awake but drowsy. Beside him, he could just make out the jade pyramid in the dark. Perched on the cabinet by his bed, it looked sleek and ready. Getting up on one elbow, Luke glanced guiltily towards Malc's faint flashing light and then reached out towards the ornament. Almost at once, he hesitated and withdrew his arm. Confused, he snuggled down again.

Laying his head back on the pillow, he listened to the slow drumbeat of blood in the region of his left ear. In the night-time gloom, he wondered how the world would react if that pulse faded away. What would Jade do? How would his newfound parents deal with another loss? Would it bring them together again or tear them apart completely? Would the world miss him or would it just go on as it always had? One thing was for sure. With a wiped memory, Malc would never think of him again. His mobile would be assigned to a new forensic investigator and carry on as if Luke Harding had never existed.

Luke sighed and told himself not to be silly. He guessed that he was being plagued by morbid thoughts because he was spending so much time in hospital among the ill, the dying and the dead.

Even though Luke had turned away from the pyramid, he could almost feel its presence. Maybe he'd pluck up the courage to use it tomorrow night. It would be futile for fixing a headache and blurry vision, of course, but it couldn't do any harm – apart from making him feel humiliated for falling back on superstition.

When Luke woke up properly on Sunday morning, he was surprised to find himself lying on top of the bed, still fully dressed. He gazed at Malc and groaned. "Better order me two pomegranates," he muttered, dragging himself upright and running a hand through his untidy hair. "The bigger, the better."

"You did not eat a main meal last night but I decided that sleep was more important than food so I did not disturb you."

"Thanks, doc." He did his best to ignore the pyramid lurking on the bedside cabinet.

After Luke had eaten breakfast and refreshed himself

in the shower, Malc announced that his father was trying to contact him. Luke grabbed the dark green pyramid and then sat down opposite the telescreen. "Okay," he said to Malc. "Put him on."

The larger-than-life version of Peter Sachs seemed to be in a good mood. "Mystery solved," he declared. "Thanks to your mother."

"Oh, good," Luke replied. "That's how I like my mysteries — solved. But which mystery are we talking about?"

Peter laughed. "You asked me if I've got a genetically identical brother — a twin. I haven't. But, in a way, I have. I'm not the only one with my DNA."

Luke sat up straight and frowned. "How do you mean?"

"I'd forgotten all about it, but Elisa reminded me. I donated my bone marrow to a leukaemia patient a few years back. Or maybe it was aplastic anaemia. Either way, he's got my bone marrow. Bob's your uncle."

Luke smiled at hearing one of his own favourite sayings coming out of his father's mouth. Perhaps he'd learned it from Peter before he'd gone to school. But he refused to be distracted. "So, does that mean this man churns out the same DNA as you?"

"Yes. Radiation's used to destroy a recipient's own bone marrow before a transplant. Then they're given the donor's. My bone marrow's working away inside him, making his blood. It's my blood, really, but it's in him. It'll have DNA identical to mine. His hair and skin – things like that – will be a mixture of his original genetic material and mine."

"Who was he?"

"Ah. That's the thing. I don't know. It's all done anonymously – for confidentiality."

"Can't you look it up in the hospital's records? If you're denied access, I can get into most things."

Peter took a deep breath. "It's not as simple as a restricted file. I got online this morning. There's no record of the operation. Nothing at all. I guess that means someone's wiped it out on purpose. I can assure you it happened, though."

Luke thought about it for a moment. Then he asked, "Well, who performed the operation?"

"Ah."

"What?"

"I can't remember the junior staff – it was a while ago – but the surgeon was Theo Crouch."

"Right. I'll go and see him, get it confirmed—"

Peter interrupted. "You can go and see him but you won't get anything out of him. He stopped work when he went down with Alzheimer's."

"There's got to be something solid if I'm going to convince Malc. Can't you tell me anything about the patient?"

Peter mumbled, "I do someone a favour and. . . now

this." He cocked his head on one side while he thought about it. "He'll have been under fifty at the time. Older people aren't recommended for bone-marrow replacement because the mortality rate goes flying up. He'll have tissue compatible with mine. That's why I would've been chosen. I must have been a good match to reduce the risk that his body would reject the transplant. I suppose he'll still be taking immunosuppressant drugs to stop it happening now." Peter's image on the wall shrugged. "That's about it."

"Well, it's something, I suppose."

"It's an explanation for my DNA turning up where I've never been."

"I'm afraid I need your pretend twin to prove that," Luke replied. "It's not so much a mystery solved as another lead."

"There's one more thing," Peter added. "I checked with Tara. Nyree Max had real transcranial direct current stimulation, not a placebo."

"Thanks," Luke replied. "You've given me plenty to think about — and follow up. Before you break the connection. . ." He turned to one side and picked up the jade pyramid. "Here it is. Remember? I told you it's supposed to make people better."

Luke's father peered at the picture on his own screen and then snorted. "Unless it's got something packed inside. . ." He shrugged. "Probably provides all the benefits of looking at a nice object. It makes you forget for a while how bad you're feeling."

Chapter Fourteen

Luke was convinced that the pyramid was solid. It was too heavy to be hollow. Even so, he turned it upside down to look for a hidden opening in the base. There was nothing. He put it down on one of its shiny sides and stepped back. "Scan it, Malc. Is it solid? Could there be anything inside?"

Hovering over the ornament, Malc examined it first in the visible region of the electromagnetic spectrum. Then he tried infrared radiation, ultraviolet light and X-rays. When he'd used every available scan, he reported, "The object appears to have been formed from a single piece of natural jadeite. I calculate from its height and the area of its base that it has a volume of 707.1 cubic centimetres. This material is known to have a density of 3.3 grams per cubic centimetre. Therefore, if it is solid jadeite, its mass should be 2.333 kilograms to the nearest gram." Malc hovered over the pyramid and scooped it up briefly on his scales. "Its mass is 2.334 kilograms, which is within experimental error."

"It's nothing but jade, then."

"Highly likely. However, you should note that my spectroscopic examination of the base has detected some specks of a dark solid."

"What is it?"

"Unknown. I can do further tests in a darkened room."

Clutching the pyramid but keeping his fingers away from its base, Luke headed for the bathroom straight away. He put it down on the surface beside the sink and said, "I'll leave you to get on with it."

"If I identify the traces, I cannot enter the result into the case notes because the origin of the substance is unknown. It may be contamination from any one of a large number of sources."

"I know. But I still want you to check it out."

Left alone, Malc analysed the marks with a fluorescence technique. He sprayed phthaldialdehyde onto the dull surface and then swept intense ultraviolet light across it and detected tiny glistening spots typical of blood proteins. Then he performed cross-over electrophoresis with antibodies from some common species and found that the proteins on the pyramid reacted only with human antibodies. Emerging from the bathroom, Malc announced, "I have detected dried human blood on the base of the jade pyramid. It is too degraded for DNA analysis."

"Human blood," Luke muttered to himself.

"Confirmed, but its origin is unidentified."

Luke pushed his hair behind his ears with both hands and let out a long breath. "Interesting, though."

"It is a conspicuous but unhelpful finding."

"Has it been there long?"

"Unknown. However, the degree of decomposition suggests that staining occurred several days ago."

Luke nodded. "This morning's all about blood. What do you make of my father's idea? Could there really be someone else going around with his blood and DNA?"

"The suspect's account is feasible, but Dr Sachs offered no proof that he has been a bone-marrow donor."

"But, if he was, that'd explain the DNA around Julian Bent and Charlie Illingworth, wouldn't it?"

"If the transplant took place, either the donor or the recipient would be responsible for the traces. In such an unusual situation, the possibility of wrongful arrest would be substantial."

"Mmm. Well, I reckon you can rule my father out."

"On what basis?"

"He wouldn't have deleted the medical record if he was going to blame a bone-marrow patient. That file would be his alibi. It's much more likely the recipient wiped it out. With no evidence that the operation ever happened, everyone would think the DNA belongs to the donor, and only the donor."

"Speculation."

"Yeah. But it makes sense."

"Dr Sachs is very clever. He could have removed the details of the transplant to prompt such speculation."

Luke winced. "That's one twist too many."

"The operation he described might not have taken

place at all. He might have invented it as a false lead."

Luke could not deny the possibility.

"It is all speculation," Malc concluded, "because you have not established that a crime has taken place. Despite this, you should note that Dr Sachs would have had many opportunities to manipulate hospital records whereas a patient would not."

Luke still didn't believe it, but Malc was right about one thing. Luke needed something more solid than guesswork. "See if you can get a list of everyone in York who's taking immunosuppressant drugs."

"Processing. This task may be prolonged if there are several different suppliers of the drugs."

"All right." Changing direction, Luke asked, "Is the Institute of Biomechanical Research open today? And is Oscar Hislop in it? I want to know what he was up to yesterday."

Malc found the information within a minute. "There is always at least one member of staff in the Institute of Biomechanical Research because human tissue can become available at any time," he said. "The officer on duty is required to assess the value of any corpse, and then express an interest in it or reject it. The officer staffing the institute today is not Oscar Hislop. He will report for work tomorrow."

Luke smiled wryly. "A day off! I wouldn't mind one of those, but I'd better talk to Crawford Gallagher and

Nyree Max about the blood on the pyramid. I'll visit the Children's Ward as well. That's where Nyree met the Heather Man. Maybe someone there knows him. First, though, I'm going to talk to Jade. Get me a link, please."

Luke laughed when he saw his girlfriend on the telescreen. For once, she looked bleary eyed. "Heavy night, eh?"

She nodded. "Ever since people got to know I'm the musician for the International Youth Games, the crowds at my gigs have doubled. I get more bookings and they go on a lot longer."

"You're in demand."

"Yeah. Like a forensic investigator who keeps getting it right." Jade took a drink from a mug. "How's tricks?"

"What's that you're drinking?"

"Hot chocolate, from York. The best in the world. You'd better bring me some back."

"I'll see what I can do, but I wanted to ask you something," he said. "If you had a stunner of a headache and someone said there was a wonder cure for it, would you take it?"

Jade didn't hesitate. "Of course I would. Nothing to lose."

"What if science said it couldn't possibly work? What if every doctor in the land agreed it was nonsense?"

"Doctors and science understand everything, do they? No. If there's a wonder cure, I'd still want it. Let's face it,

I can't explain what makes a really good piece of music, but I don't let it stop me trying for that bit of magic." Jade rubbed her eyes with both hands. "But this isn't about me. It's about you, FI Harding. You're still bad."

Luke shook his head, even though the hammers were still pounding the inside of his skull.

Jade ignored his gesture. "What's this wonder cure you've got?"

"It's silly, really," Luke answered. "Do you remember Nyree Max coming in to see me at hospital? She was carrying a green pyramid."

"Yeah. A little girl. She said the pyramid cured her." She took another gulp of hot chocolate and then beamed at Luke. "She also said jade's good for you."

"That's the one."

"It's her magic pyramid you've got, then."

"It's right over there," he said, nodding towards the table.

"What are you waiting for?"

"It's got some dried blood on it."

Jade shrugged. "So what? You're just inventing excuses. Nyree nicked her finger and spilled a drop on it. Something like that. Use it, Luke. What's the worst that can happen? People will rubbish it. That's all. What do they know? Anyway, they're not the ones with the pain in their heads. You are. And you didn't ask for it, did you? You didn't give it permission to invade you. It just came anyway. I think you're entitled to kick it out any way you can."

"Hmm."

Jade put on a stern voice. "You always let your brain rule. This time, give it a rest. Sounds like it needs one. Ignore your brain and. . . like. . . go with your heart."

"My heart's a pump. That's all. It doesn't rule anything, apart from my pulse."

"You sound like Malc. You know what I mean. Give it a go. Okay?"

Unable to refuse her, he nodded. "All right. Tonight maybe."

"Definitely."

Chapter Fifteen

Walking towards Crawford Gallagher's riverside shack, Luke felt more upbeat. A chat with Jade normally did the trick, even when she talked nonsense about a trinket like the pyramid.

Spotting Gallagher coming in the opposite direction, Luke made an instant decision to follow him. Luke turned his back and headed for a launch moored to the bank. Boarding the motorboat, he squatted down and ordered Malc to hide behind the boat's control room. After Crawford had ambled past, blind to the forensic investigator and Mobile Aid to Law and Crime, Luke stood up again. "Come on," he whispered to Malc. "Covert surveillance mode."

At the bridge, Crawford turned up Museum Walkway, heading for the city centre.

Luke lingered behind, an anonymous figure among many, while Malc kept tabs on the artist by moving from building to building above and behind the target.

Dressed formally in a dark suit, white shirt and red tie, Crawford stopped outside York Theatre, possibly to get his breath back, possibly to check if anyone was following him. The old man did not think to look up to where Malc's video system was recording his behaviour. On the opposite side of the busy corridor stood the York Mint.

Inside the grand building, workers churned out identity cards for most of northern England.

Luke leaned stealthily against the wall of the City Hall's Registry Department and waited.

Instead of crossing over towards the Mint, Crawford checked that no one was paying him any attention and then slipped furtively down an alleyway behind the theatre.

Luke did not dare to make a move. If he followed the healer, Crawford was certain to notice him in such a narrow passageway. He just had to hope that Malc was in a position to monitor what Crawford was doing.

Two minutes later, Malc returned obediently to Luke's side. "The target has entered a disused structure. You can pursue him without being seen."

"Show me."

As soon as Luke turned off the main freeway, he found himself in a dank alley. At the end of it, there was a rickety door with a padlock. Reaching it, Luke hesitated and scratched his head. "First obstacle."

"The subject did not seem to use a key," Malc told him.

"Oh." Luke put out his right hand and grabbed the padlock. Immediately, the whole contraption – padlock and staple – swung free. It was in place only for show. Cautiously, Luke pushed the door inwards and let sunlight penetrate the interior.

He expected to see a derelict room but he was wrong.

Narrow stone steps led down to a dark tunnel. The ancient steps were so worn that they had become curved in shape. Luke shrugged. "Oh well. Here goes."

By the time he'd taken two steps, the door swung shut behind him and he was left in total darkness. "Minimum light, Malc. Just so I can see a few metres ahead."

Malc provided a faint beam and said, "For security, I will go first."

"All right. Minimum sound level as well, please."

At the bottom of the long series of steps, a grim subway went to the right. The suffocating cave seemed to burrow under the theatre. There was only one way to go, so Luke had to be following Crawford Gallagher, but there was no sign of him.

Malc manoeuvred himself carefully so that he did not scrape against the brick walls on either side. Luke stooped a little because the ceiling was not far above his head.

"Is this tunnel marked on any of your maps of the city?" Luke asked in a whisper.

Malc consulted his databases while he led the way. "No."

"I wonder where we're going."

"I calculate that we are now under High Petergate Corridor."

"Perhaps we're in Low Petergate Corridor," Luke replied with a grin.

This secret, subterranean part of York was a complete

contrast with the lively city above ground. Water trickled down one wall. It was probably more than water because it had a foul smell. Luke went past the stream and the stench as quickly as he could. In front of him, the bleak subway still stretched. It was not quite straight, though. Crawford must have been hidden from Luke by the slight curve. If the old man was familiar with the passageway, he'd be able to move along it a lot quicker than Luke. Maybe he'd already reached whatever lay ahead.

A minute later, Malc went under a thick arch of bricks. "Using the distance and direction that we have come, I compute that we are now entering the basement of York Mint," he announced at low volume.

Luke ducked under the archway and paused. "Stop here. Silent mode. And turn your light off."

It was even creepier in the dark, like being buried alive. But it served its purpose. Somewhere ahead, there was a dim glow. There were also voices, too distant for Luke to distinguish words. "Record it all, Malc," he whispered to his mobile. "I'm going nearer."

With every step, taken carefully without making a sound, the subway became lighter and wider. With every step, Luke was closer to making sense of the voices.

121

Chapter Sixteen

The subway opened out into a vault under York Mint. Luke and Malc used one of the sturdy stone pillars that held up the building to conceal themselves from the small gathering in the centre of the chamber. Above the group, a long fluorescent tube set in the rough ceiling provided a soft light.

Luke recognized Crawford's voice saying, "I believe God works through my art. Understand? He heals through me." He sounded both stubborn and frustrated.

A stern reply echoed around the crypt. "We're humans, Crawford. That's all. We don't presume to interfere with God's good work. The sick must ask for His mercy and His forgiveness. They must place themselves in His hands, not the hands of doctors or healers."

A woman added, "God alone decides who should live with sickness — with punishment. It's a sin not to trust His judgement in this. You must live in harmony with Him, not against Him."

"That's what I'm saying," Crawford replied, even more agitated. "You see, that's exactly what I do. He guides my hand. I'm sure of it."

"A bold claim, Crawford. Very bold."

Luke was familiar with the group's peculiar ideas about an all-powerful supernatural being. He'd heard the same views when he'd infiltrated The World Church of Eternal Vision as part of his Lost Bullet case. Clearly, he had gate-crashed a meeting of the York Chapter of the illegal organization. And Luke knew that Visionaries, as they called themselves, had an alarming way of testing faith in the church.

"If you're right," the woman said, "if you're in harmony with God and the Angels, you'll be in harmony with every one of His creatures. The time's come, Crawford."

The human voices quietened. The vault hushed.

Luke did not have to peer around the pillar to know what was happening. Back in November, when he'd joined the church, he'd participated in the test. Crawford Gallagher would be removing his jacket, baring his forearm and placing it within striking distance of a poisonous rattlesnake.

Luke tensed when he heard the reptile's fearsome rattle, like the shake of a handful of gravel. The noise was the terrifying prelude to a bite.

An unseen Visionary gasped and a gentle voice said, "The Angels protect those who are at one with God and nature."

If Luke broke cover now, he knew that the startled snake was bound to strike the nearest person. He had to stay out of sight and hope that Crawford passed the outlandish test.

But Luke's wish was shattered by a scream.

At once, Luke came out from behind one side of the pillar. Taking his lead from Luke, Malc emerged from the other. Crawford was on his knees, staring in shock at the blood and fang marks on his bare left arm. The congregation took one look at the forensic investigator with his mobile and ran off in the opposite direction. The rattlesnake slithered towards Luke but stopped beside Crawford's legs. It seemed to be guarding its victim.

Luke ignored the Visionaries scurrying away. More concerned for Crawford, he edged his way towards the healer and, at the same time, said, "Send an emergency message to the poison unit, Malc. I need an anti-venom team here. Now."

"Transmitting."

One of the most dangerous animals in the world, the rattlesnake was pale brown with dark diamond shapes along its body. Alert, it kept its flattened head up and fixed its sinister eyes on Luke. It seemed to regard him as a rival predator. It flicked out its tongue as if licking its lips.

Luke stopped a few metres away from Crawford and the rattler. He was thinking through his options when Malc announced, "I cannot risk your health." In the gloomy chamber, a bright laser beam flashed. The snake did not stand a chance. It writhed for a second and then fell in a limp coil.

Luke dashed forward and grabbed Crawford's shirt

sleeve in both fists. He ripped it apart to make sure that it didn't constrict the blood flow near the bite, where the swelling would begin within five minutes.

Crawford was stunned, unable to talk. His teeth had locked together in a grimace. By now, his arm would be aflame with extreme pain.

"What are his chances, Malc?"

"His chances of what?" the mobile asked.

"Of being okay."

"Very good if the anti-venom is administered within an hour, or two hours at most. Amputation should not be necessary. However, respiratory failure is a possibility."

"There must be a way out over there," Luke said, pointing. "Where the others ran. Maybe it's a better way in for the anti-venom unit. Check it, Malc."

Left alone with Crawford, Luke examined the dead snake. Malc had drilled a neat hole right through its head. It wasn't messy like a wound inflicted by a bullet. The intense light had burned its way through the reptile's tissue, leaving clear entrance and exit holes. Luke moved its coils to one side with his foot.

Still silent, Crawford was sweating profusely. The muscles in his bare arm and face were twitching eerily. Without warning, he crumpled onto the grubby floor.

Luke could do nothing more for Crawford Gallagher. The stricken healer was being treated in the Poisoning Unit.

If the artist had been younger, he would have been expected to make a complete and rapid recovery from the snake venom. But the chemical shock and intense pain had taken a severe toll on Crawford's elderly body. Luke could only wait while the specialists worked on him.

Luke used the time to visit the Children's Ward. On the way, Malc told him, "I have sent my images of the members of The World Church of Eternal Vision to The Authorities. You are not required to find these people and charge them with belonging to an illegal society. The Authorities will assign another FI to the task so that you can concentrate on the hospital case."

"Fair enough," he replied, entering the ward where Nyree had stayed.

The first patient that Luke saw was a boy who had cranked his bed up to its maximum height and made a pretend-camp underneath it.

While Luke watched and smiled, the ward supervisor said, "He's a lot happier underneath it than sleeping on top, so why not? It's like an adventure for him. Anything to make their time here more fun. Most bring their toys in."

Luke nodded. "Talking of toys, you discharged a girl with a pyramid last Monday. Do you remember? It was a sort of lucky charm."

"Nyree Max. Crippling migraines. She'd be totally incapacitated by her attacks."

"That's right. How did you cure her?"

"Well, it wasn't her pyramid, for sure. She had an experimental drug. The doctor would tell you all about it, if you want, but it's been effective for a lot of patients. It's flying through its clinical trial." The supervisor hesitated. "Oh, yes. She also had brain stimulation. It's something new and alternative."

"Do you know the Heather Man?" Luke asked.

"I've never seen him in here."

"Nyree said she met him. Not this time. On her previous stay."

The supervisor shrugged.

"I don't suppose you know who he is, do you?"

"Not a clue."

"Nor me," Luke replied with a sigh.

"One thing's for sure. He doesn't seem interested in kids much. That's unusual, I guess."

"Mmm. Thanks," said Luke. "Good point." But he wasn't sure if it was significant.

In the waiting room outside the Poisoning Unit, Luke requested a sound link to Nyree Max. As soon as his mobile provided it, Luke asked, "Did you look at the bottom of your pyramid?"

"Yes. Why?"

"What was on it?"

"Nothing," Nyree answered. "It was black and. . . sort

of empty."

"Did you cut yourself at all while you had it?"

"Er. . . no."

"Certain?"

"Yeah."

"Is there any way you might've got blood on its base?"

"I don't think so," she replied. "No."

"All right," said Luke. "Thanks again."

A nurse came into the waiting area with the news that Luke wouldn't be able to speak to Crawford Gallagher for at least twenty-four hours. The doctors were still worried about possible heart failure. And, anyway, the patient wasn't capable of talking.

Instead, Luke went to search for answers in the artist's shack. Normally he would examine a suspect's computer for incriminating information, but in this case, Crawford didn't have one. Somehow, that didn't surprise Luke. Gallagher didn't seem to be the type to keep records. His cluttered displays and workbench didn't reveal anything significant. Finally, Luke went through the old man's waste bin. And that's when his search paid off.

He held up a small glass vial between his gloved forefinger and thumb. The screw-cap container was missing its top and it had been washed out thoroughly. Luke put it down carefully on a clean part of the bench and said, "Check if there's anything left inside, Malc."

Positioning himself over the vial, Malc carried out

chemical analyses until he had the answer. "The vial contains a trace of dried human blood."

"Like the bottom of the pyramid," Luke muttered, almost to himself.

"Correct. The surface of this counter has similar tiny stains. However, it is not possible to determine if the blood stains have the same source because of decomposition and shortage of sample."

"Pity."

Luke looked out of the back window, watching the activity on the busy river, as he thought about the healer and his pyramid. "Makes you wonder what he meant when he told me to use the pyramid and then take it back to him so he could recharge its batteries."

"The jade pyramid does not have batteries."

"Exactly," Luke replied.

Chapter Seventeen

In his room on Sunday night, Luke left his bedside lamp on. In front of it stood the tall ornament, casting a long cool shadow across his pillow. Sitting up in bed, Luke reached out and took its weight in both hands. Nearly two and a half kilograms. "It's a lump of jade," he told himself. "Jade's jade, not medicine." But Crawford Gallagher said it would heal. Nyree Max believed in it and Jade wanted him to give it a try. Ridiculous. It couldn't have any effect on his health. At least that meant it couldn't make his head worse.

Slowly, Luke brought one of the smooth surfaces towards his left ear, just as Crawford had shown him. Then he replaced the pyramid on the cabinet in front of the lamp. He settled down with the ornament's shadow falling across him like an ominous black dagger. As he drifted into sleep, he was convinced that he was making a complete fool of himself. Still, his mobile was the only witness to his madness and Malc wouldn't tell anyone else.

It was Monday and Luke woke at seven o'clock when the rising sun made his curtains bright yellow. Several streaks of daylight punctured the gaps around the material. One beam shone directly onto Luke's face. He blinked and shifted his position. His first sight was Malc. It almost always was. Next, he focused on the sleek pyramid. Sitting up against the pillow, he felt the side of his head. The pain was still there. Of course it was. How could a trinket make it better?

He moaned and murmured, "Just as bad."

"The pyramid should have triggered the placebo effect but, in your case, it has not," said Malc.

In the sunlight, Luke could hardly tell that his bedside lamp was still switched on. He swung his long legs over the side of the mattress. "A placebo's just pretending to treat someone." He still hoped that in time his own body would repair whatever was wrong. If he had to take his father's advice and check in to a health centre, he'd do it once he'd finished his investigation.

"The placebo effect is more complicated than that. Research proves that it is real and positive. Patients experiencing pain report a lessening of their symptoms when they are given imitation tablets that have no painkilling effect. Medical scans show that, in response to the dummy treatment, their brains release the natural painkilling substances called endorphins."

Wrapping himself in a warm dressing gown, Luke said, "So, anticipating relief makes it happen?"

"Confirmed. Medical science has not yet explained the mechanism but it is genuine because it can be measured. It is considered by many doctors to be a powerful factor

for healing human beings. However, it is effective only in people who have faith that they will benefit by their treatment. You did not."

Luke smiled wryly. "The body's an amazing thing."

"There is interplay between a person's state of mind and the physical body. For example, sadness activates the tear glands and fear stimulates the sweat glands. When a human feels angry or embarrassed, the face goes red because the body widens the blood vessels. In the placebo effect, an optimistic frame of mind releases endorphins."

"So, if I felt positive about a cure – no matter how crazy – I'd get a feel-good factor because my brain would pump out painkillers?"

"Correct. Some experiments suggest that the placebo effect increases as the treatment becomes more bizarre."

Luke went through to the living quarters. "You're saying healing's a mixture of mind games and medicine."

"That appears to be true."

Once Luke had eaten a pomegranate breakfast and taken a shower, he was keen to continue his case. It was too early to see Crawford Gallagher in the Poisoning Unit so he decided to return to the Institute of Biomechanical Research instead. Before he set out, though, he placed the pyramid in a bag and took it with him.

On the way, Malc announced his latest findings. "I have a list of all York residents taking immunosuppressant drugs. There are currently one hundred and twenty-four such patients."

Luke was disappointed. He'd hoped that there would be fewer patients to pursue in an attempt to prove that his father had been a bone-marrow donor. "Check all their medical records, Malc. I want to know which ones are taking the pills because they've had a bone-marrow transplant."

"Processing."

In the main refrigerated laboratory of the Institute of Biomechanical Research, a sledge with a human head attached to it flew forwards at high speed and crashed into a sturdy pane of glass. The thick window withstood the sickening collision but the skull cracked.

"Two days ago," Oscar Hislop said proudly, "it was attached to a woman, but now it's got thirty sensors embedded in it to measure impact injury to the skull and brain." For a few seconds, the biomechanical researcher studied the recordings on his computer monitor. When he looked up, he seemed satisfied. The experiment had clearly given him the data that he wanted. "Not very dignified for her, I guess," he said, nodding towards the sledge, "but she's served humanity. Maybe saved a lot of lives when we analyse the results. I'd better not tell you what we're doing with the rest of her body."

Luke found it hard not to wince. He didn't look at the damaged head with sensors inside and out. "Do you ever need slices of human brain?" he asked.

"Of course. Slippery things." Oscar pointed to a machine in the corner of the room. "We put a brain in there and it cuts slices of precise thicknesses." He paused and added with a grim smile, "That's when we're not using it to slice beef for the canteen." He looked at Luke and said, "No. That's a joke. We'd never do that. Ham's a different matter, though."

Oscar seemed to need an offhand manner to get him through the day but Luke couldn't laugh along with him. Unlike the biomechanical engineer, Luke hadn't become hardened to the disturbing activities in the research institute. He didn't want to become hardened like Oscar Hislop. "What do you use brain slices for?"

"A couple of things. We've got what you might call a squishometer. We're comparing the squishiness of normal tissue with brains that've got a tumour. One day, we'll be able to wiggle someone's body and look for cancer because tumours are at least ten times stiffer than healthy tissue. If something doesn't jiggle around like jelly, it might well be cancer."

"You said there was something else."

"Ah, yes. My pet project. It's a high-intensity ultrasonic probe. It almost boils cancer cells, killing them outright, but doesn't touch normal ones. And it's non-invasive. It works from outside the body. Very promising. It could be the future for treating awkward tumours. It's like shaking them to bits with loud music."

Luke suspected that Oscar was a caring person. Otherwise, he wouldn't be working in this chilling and chilly laboratory. But he'd had to put sentimentality aside to do his important and unsavoury job. As unemotional as Malc, he was treating human body parts like a butcher handled meat. Luke was also wondering if Oscar regarded a supply of organs for his research as more important than living donors. Maybe, to be so caring, he'd had to switch off his humanity altogether. That would be some paradox.

"Do you always have to use real bodies?" said Luke.

"No. Take a look at this." Oscar led the way to a small room at normal temperature. On a table was a mushy model of human innards. "Do you want to put your hand in? It's a synthetic model of the human abdomen, complete with pretend-blood flow. We can even generate nasty smells when we want to fake a perforated intestine. You see, when surgeons remove a spleen, they do it with hands and fingers. This is great for medical students to practise on. It mimics all the squidgy bits of the guts." With considerable relish, he added, "It feels exactly like putting your hands into a real human body."

"Mmm. I'll give it a miss, if you don't mind," said Luke. But he was relieved to see that Oscar could at least be enthusiastic about something that hadn't once been alive.

A technician dressed head-to-foot in a white overall

emerged from the side room and began to wipe away threads attached to her clothing.

Seeing Luke's curiosity, Oscar explained, "That's the spider room. Nothing in it but spiders spinning webs."

"What for?"

"Spider silk's the strongest natural fibre, you know. You can sterilize it with heat and use it for surgical stitching or repairing tendons. We're looking at genetically engineered spiders as well. We've added genes that make their silk really stiff. You can grow human cells on it and implant it in people to repair bones. Anyone who's scared of spiders is going to have to rethink."

Luke brought him back to his human experiments. "Have you ever had to go scouting for brain tissue?"

"You asked me on Saturday," Oscar replied. "A tactful memo normally does the job."

"So, what happens when it doesn't? What do you do if you need something that's not available?"

Oscar shrugged. "What can we do? We wait. We've learned to be good at waiting."

"You don't try to accelerate things?"

For a moment, Oscar pretended that he didn't understand. Then he said, "Of course not. I told you, we're very respectful."

"So, you didn't go to the Brain Injury Unit on Saturday afternoon?"

Showing discomfort for the first time, Oscar looked

down at his shuffling feet. Then he said, "Oh, yes. Sorry. I still put respect top of the list but, yes, I went to have a quiet word with a contact after work. It's not a regular thing. I just needed a bit of advance warning about the availability of a cancerous brain. You know. So I can plan the tests. Let's be honest. I owe it to the donor to get the best possible results out of it and to do that I need a bit of forward planning."

Luke nodded. He had proved that Oscar had lied to further his biomechanical research. What else might he do?

Leaving the upsetting institute, Luke said to Malc, "I need some fresh air. I don't know how Hislop and his staff stand it."

"People in harrowing jobs often cope by using dark humour."

"Yeah," Luke agreed. "Not that you'd understand it."

"Correct, but I am aware that it is a feature of human psychology."

"Mmm. Sometimes they just go crazy. Oscar might be funny and kind – and a killer. Or it might be one of his workmates. So, check if the Brain Injury Unit's had any deaths since he called in."

After a minute, the mobile replied, "No fatalities reported."

"Good. I can try a different angle, then. You remember that motor-neurone-disease patient we were told about on Saturday afternoon? Sandy Chipperfield. She had a bunch of heather and she was sent home."

"I have a recording of the conversation."

"Okay. Find out where she lived, please. I'm going to pay a visit."

"She is deceased."

"Yeah. I mean visit her partner, friends or neighbours. And check out anything else she took away from the hospital. Let's face it. She's still one of the hospital's fatalities even if she died after she got home."

Chapter Eighteen

In the electric cab, Malc informed Luke that he had whittled down the long list of people taking immunosuppressant drugs to four patients who'd had a bone-marrow transplant.

"That's more like it," Luke replied. "I can cope with four. How many are men?"

"Three."

Luke's father had said that he'd had the operation a few years ago and, at the time, the bone-marrow recipient would have been fifty years old at most. Luke asked, "How many of them are under sixty?"

"Two."

"Even better. Why did they need bone marrow?"

"Both were leukaemia patients."

The cab slowed outside Sandy Chipperfield's house. "Okay," said Luke. "Store their details. I want to follow them up after this."

The apartment had clearly been neglected in the past few days, probably since Sandy had died. It hadn't been cleaned or tidied. There was a lot of dirty crockery and cutlery on the dinner table. Obviously, Sandy's grieving partner had more on his mind than household chores. Fidgeting like a hyperactive child, Marvin stood beside a specialized music centre and shuffled from foot to foot. "You feel this crushing weight when it happens," he said. "Absolutely terrible. And ironic. She was a dancer, you know, but she could hardly move at all at the end." He sat down but, unable to settle, he got up again and prowled back and forth. "She was never much good with words. That's not how she expressed herself. Sandy communicated through her body and movement. The disease robbed her of her life. Not just because it killed her. It's crueller than that. It took away her reason for living. She couldn't dance."

Luke offered the only words that he could find. "I'm sorry."

"Her doctor said there was no reason for her to die when she did but. . ." He sighed heavily. "It was always going to happen soon. No getting away from that."

"So, her doctor was surprised?"

"He thought she'd have more time. Not quality time – the opposite. She'd just get worse and worse. He said I should be grateful she went quickly. Less suffering that way."

"How long was it after she got home?"

"What's this got to do with a forensic investigator?"

"I'm just checking out hospital statistics really. Making sure everything's in order."

"Well, she passed away – I don't know – hours after she got back. It's all a blur. Less than a day."

"Did the hospital talk to you about donating any organs or her body. . ."

Marvin looked aghast. "Yes. As if I'd agree to any. . . interference." Plainly appalled by the thought, he shook his head firmly.

"Did she bring anything back with her from hospital?"

Marvin looked puzzled. "The wheelchair, do you mean?"

"Anything else?"

"No. Except. . ."

"What?"

"A bunch of flowers."

"What sort of flowers?" Luke asked.

"Heather. I don't know where they came from. It wasn't me."

"Have you still got them?"

Marvin waved towards a bedroom door.

"Do you mind if I take a look?"

"Help yourself," Marvin answered.

The bedroom had not been cleared. The wheelchair lay abandoned in one corner. A thick chequered blanket was draped over its arms. In the opposite corner, Sandy's death had been marked by the traditional show of lilies. On top of a chest of drawers, the bunch of heather was lying on its side, going brown and brittle. A pile of clothes sat untidily on a chair beside the bed.

"Scan, please, Malc. Especially the wheelchair and

141

heather."

Out of the bedroom window, there was a view of the skyline of York. At this distance, Luke couldn't make out the glass pods at the top of the big wheel. The arch that was visible above the buildings looked like a simple metallic skeleton.

"The heather is composed entirely of dead *Erica carnea*. Within the parameters you specified, there is only one finding of interest. Some particles adhering to the blanket are biscuit crumbs."

Luke spun round. "Don't tell me! They're made of oats and linseed."

Malc did not reply.

"Well?"

"You instructed me not to respond."

"No, I mean. . . never mind. What are they made of?"

"The main ingredients are flour, oats, desiccated coconut and linseed."

"Much the same as the ones in Julian Bent's room," said Luke.

"Confirmed. I am also attempting to identify one minor ingredient."

"What sort of ingredient?"

"It is a seed."

"All right. Carry on," Luke said as he made for the living room. Watching Marvin carefully, he asked, "Did you give Sandy any biscuits?"

"Biscuits? No. Why?"

"If my mobile searched your kitchen, he wouldn't find flour, oats, desiccated coconut and linseed, then?"

"Flour and oats, yes. Not the others. But why are you. . .?"

Luke was convinced that Sandy's partner was genuinely baffled by his questions. "I think Sandy ate a biscuit while she had that blanket wrapped round her."

Marvin was perturbed now. "What are you getting at?"

"Nothing. I just need to know if someone's been handing round biscuits at the hospital."

"Well, she didn't get it here, so they must've been. And I'll tell you this," Marvin said, "Sandy would've needed help to eat it."

As soon as Luke stepped out of Sandy Chipperfield's quarters, Malc reported, " I have a highly significant result that you would not have wanted me to discuss in the presence of the victim's partner."

Luke hesitated before he called for a cab to take him back to the hospital. "Victim?"

"It is highly likely that Julian Bent and Sandy Chipperfield were murdered."

"What have you come up with?"

"I have identified the additional seed as a castor bean, *Ricinus communis*."

Luke took a deep breath. Every forensic investigator

knew about castor beans. They formed a part of every criminology course. The seeds of the castor-oil plant were infamous because they were the source of a poison that was lethal at levels below the detection limits of all forensic tests. One thousandth of a gram of ricin was enough to kill a human being. Luke recalled one of his instructors telling him that two beans would be fatal if the victim released the ricin by chewing them – and that pathology would never be able to detect the poison.

Standing beside the cab tracks, Luke nodded slowly. "Inform The Authorities, Malc. Looks like I've got a multiple murder case."

"Transmitting."

"Remind me. What are the symptoms of ricin poisoning?"

"A burning sensation in the mouth, throat and stomach, sickness, abdominal cramps, convulsions, internal bleeding, breathing difficulty, and death."

"Mmm. Maybe not enough to be noticed in people who are already weak and sick. How long before curtains?"

Malc took a moment to analyse the question and then replied, "I cannot answer. Interpretation error."

"Curtains means the end. Death. How long does ricin take to kill?"

"The time interval is variable. Loss of life can occur within a few hours or up to twelve days after ingestion.

You should also know that my database includes four previous cases of castor beans used as a murder weapon by mixing with linseed in cakes or biscuits. It is very effective unless the food is heated prior to consumption, because high temperature destroys ricin. None of these past cases occurred recently or in this area. The latter three took place after a news bulletin featured details of the first case."

"So, the information's out there for anyone to copy."

"Confirmed."

"Does the castor-oil plant grow in this country?"

"Not naturally. It is common in tropical climates."

"Greenhouse conditions might do it. Did you see any sign of it at Crawford Gallagher's place?"

"No."

At last, Luke swept his identity card through the trackside reader and announced his destination as York Hospital. Then he turned back to Malc and said, "Get me an urgent link to Oscar Hislop. He grabbed Charlie Illingworth's body. Find out if he's still got the stomach and intestines. I want their contents analysed as a priority job. I know you didn't spot any bits of biscuit on the body but I still want to know the last thing Charlie ate."

Chapter Nineteen

Luke placed his bag on the seat of the cab and then put his sore head in his hands for a moment. When he looked up, he said, "Here I am, calling for someone to poke around in a dead man's guts. Most people of my age wouldn't even know the contents of stomachs and intestines get analysed. But I do."

"Having been trained, you cannot be untrained," Malc replied with infallible logic but no understanding of Luke's unease.

Luke had only a few minutes of rest before the cab delivered him to the hospital's reception. Wasting no time, he dashed to the Poisoning Unit to check on Crawford Gallagher's status. The nurse on duty gave him good news. The patient was conscious, improving and ready for brief visits.

When Luke walked into his room, the old man's eyes opened. "You," he muttered.

Luke nodded and smiled. "Yeah, me. Here," he said, as he took the jade pyramid out of the bag and set it on Crawford's bedside cabinet. "You'll have faith in this." Hiding his own disbelief, he added, "It'll help you recover."

Crawford shook his head. "You've used it. It needs recharging."

"And how do you do that?"

Crawford looked away, apparently unwilling to answer.

"Does it involve blood?" Luke asked.

"How do you know. . .?"

"Whose blood?"

Crawford sighed. "The blood of the righteous. I use my own," he admitted.

Luke nodded towards the swelling on Crawford's left forearm. "The snake has made that easy enough."

The healer lifted his other arm off the bed and struggled to pull back the sleeve. The scars of past cuts between wrist and elbow were evidence that he was telling the truth.

Changing the subject, Luke said, "You grow pretty good heather. What about castor-oil plants?"

The healer shook his head again.

"Have you heard of them?"

"They're an ornamental plant in India."

Luke tried a bluff. "Someone told me you make your own biscuits. Oats, coconut, linseed and that sort of thing."

Crawford's face creased. "I don't know why anyone would tell you that. No. It's not true."

Luke shrugged. "They must have been thinking of somebody else, then. Has anyone offered you homemade biscuits in here?"

"No."

"If someone does, take them, but don't eat them. Okay? Ask a nurse to contact me straight away. It's important."

The artist nodded weakly. "They say you saved my life."

"The doctors did that. I just got them to you in time."

Looking guilty and afraid, he asked, "Are you going to ask me about the church?"

"Nothing to do with me. It's not my case." Luke was about to leave but he added, "By the way, ask the nurses to tell me if you see the Heather Man as well."

Clearly, Crawford tired easily. He was having trouble keeping his eyes open. "What was your name?"

"Luke Harding."

Barely awake, the old man muttered, "I'll pray for you."

In the hospital canteen, Luke nodded his appreciation towards the attendant who brought his lunch to the table. Then he waved his fork at Malc. "Julian, Sandy and Charlie have got something in common, you know. They all had a terminal disease. Interesting, isn't it? What's the motive for killing someone who's going to die at any moment?"

"Unknown. However, the Institute of Biomechanical Research could have been impatient to work on certain types of tissue. Murder would make material available sooner."

Luke smiled. "Material. That's what people become, is it? Material for research."

"That is the institute's point of view."

"But they didn't get their hands on Julian Bent or Sandy Chipperfield."

"Their bodies may have been earmarked for harvesting but, after death, their partners did not give permission to the research institute."

Luke nodded. "Well, it's not the transplant department trying to speed up a source of fresh organs. That theory's not holding water. No one would want organs riddled with ricin."

"Correct."

"But there is a reason for killing the near-dead. You'd know if you were human. Or humane. What if someone was doing them a favour and putting an end to their misery?"

"That is another rational motive."

Luke had been trained so thoroughly in criminology that he could almost recite the rule books. "No one has the right to take life – apart from The Authorities when they're carrying out the death sentence according to the law – but it wouldn't be classed as murder. Not quite."

"Correct," Malc replied. "Euthanasia is illegal because premature death is not a valid option for treating the terminally ill. Strictly, the crime would be categorized as assisting or enforcing suicide, depending on whether the victim or the perpetrator initiated the loss of life."

"Mmm. Giving Sandy Chipperfield a lethal biscuit and allowing her to decide whether and when to eat it would be assisting suicide, for sure. But Marvin said she would've needed help to eat it. If someone fed it to her, that's a heavy form of assisting, more like enforcing."

"You should regard Marvin as a suspect."

"Maybe, but it was her doctor who thought a quick death was a good thing. He wasn't Julian Bent's doctor as well, was he?"

"No."

"Well, he's not going to be a suspect for Julian Bent and about thirty other hospital cases. And neither's Marvin."

Luke finished a mouthful of baguette while he thought about his next move. The possibility that the hospital's odd statistics were caused by mercy killings was making him more nervous about his father. Luke had convinced himself that Peter was too caring to be capable of murder. But perhaps he cared enough to assist or enforce a suicide after life had become unbearable for a patient.

"What about those two men with leukaemia who've had bone-marrow transplants?"

Malc replied, "What do you wish to know about them?"

"I want their details – to check if either got bone marrow from my father."

"I have already eliminated one from your inquiry. His medical records name the bone-marrow donor and it is not Peter Sachs. The other patient is called Bob Beckham. He is forty-six years old and he works at York Chocolate Factory. Many details are missing from his file. It does not identify the source of his bone marrow."

"I need to speak to him, so find out where he is. While I'm here, though," Luke said, wiping his hands on a serviette, "I'd better see my father. And I suppose you'd better scan his room for biscuit crumbs."

Peter Sachs beamed when he saw Luke coming into his office. Straight away, he turned to Tara Fortune and said, "We'll sort this out another time, Tara. Okay?" Once his assistant had left without a word, he shook Luke's hand. "How are you feeling?"

"Not too bad, thanks. My main headache's this case."

Peter shook his head in disapproval. "Your other headache comes first. Shall I tell you what's bothering me?"

"What?"

"I don't dare to tell Elisa, but tumours in the brain sometimes make people produce too much human growth hormone. They grow very tall."

"Huh. I'm hardly taller than you. I bet it's all in the genes. Rebellious and tall," he said, dismissing his father's concerns. "I came to ask you about someone called Bob

151

Beckham. Does that name mean anything to you?"

"No. Should it?"

"He could be your bone-marrow man," said Luke.

"Ah. Sorry. I wouldn't know."

"I'm working on it. Right now, though, I want to ask you what you think about euthanasia."

"I'm in favour," his father answered bluntly.

"Really?"

"In some circumstances, yes. The trouble with modern medicine is, at one extreme, it can't help with some complaints. At the other, it's so effective, it prolongs life when all quality's gone. Sometimes, it extends existence well beyond what nature intended – and what patients want. So, I think there are a few cases – probably very few – where it's justified to call a halt."

While Malc roved steadily around the office, Luke asked, "Would you do it yourself, if someone begged you to?"

Peter laughed. "No. If someone's capable of begging, they haven't reached the point where their life's not worth living."

"All right. What if they begged you to do it once they got to that point?"

Peter took a deep breath. "Well, then I'd have to give it serious thought, wouldn't I?"

"It'd be illegal. A mercy killing's still killing."

"Yes, but this is more about my duty to a patient and a

fellow human being. For me, that comes before the law."

Luke wasn't surprised by Peter's response but he was disappointed. His father had just confessed to having a motive and Malc would have recorded it.

Chapter Twenty

The biscuit crumbs that Malc had detected in Dr Sachs's room were recognizable as commercial products. They did not contain the same combination of oats and seeds as the crumbs in Julian Bent's room and on Sandy Chipperfield's blanket.

Keen to know whether the stone man's death could be linked to the other two, Luke asked, "What's happening with Charlie Illingworth's body? Update, please, Malc."

"The hospital pathologist has removed the relevant innards and taken them to the laboratory where an examination is about to begin."

Luke grimaced. "Charming."

"Given that humans regard references to their entrails as distasteful, your statement must be ironic."

Luke did not reply because he felt edgy as he approached York Chocolate Factory. "When I see Bob Beckham — and anyone else to do with the case — I want you to scan for those biscuit ingredients and any sign of castor-oil plants or their seeds."

Malc replied, "Task logged."

Around the factory, the air was heavy with a smell so sweet that it was almost sickly. A crane lifted a crate of chocolate products from the rear of the large building and placed it gently on an auto-barge moored in the canal basin. Inside, Luke found the gaunt figure of Bob Beckham poking around inside a partly dismantled computer.

Luke held out his identity card. "How are you doing?"

Getting over the shock of seeing a forensic investigator, Bob put down a small pair of pliers and answered, "I've got a few years left in me yet."

Bob's frail voice did not inspire confidence, but Luke smiled anyway. "Glad to hear it."

"What do you want?"

Luke was less than half of Bob's age, but much taller. "I'm here on behalf of the hospital. It's strange that some bits of your medical notes are missing."

"Oh?"

"I was trying to find out about the source of your bone marrow, but it's not there."

Bob was wearing a regulation blue overall, like almost every worker in the chocolate factory. He hesitated for a moment and then shrugged. "Well, I don't know. It was all anonymous."

"I'll take a sample of your blood to find out."

Bob looked alarmed. "Why? The bone marrow was okay, wasn't it?"

"Yes. There's no medical problem. . ."

"That's okay, then."

"It's about record-keeping." Luke showed Bob where to place his thumb on Malc's casing so that the mobile could prick his skin and extract a tiny sample of blood. "Do you know why some of your details aren't there?"

"No idea. Nothing to do with me."

"I suppose you go into the hospital a lot. For check-ups. It's leukaemia, isn't it?"

Bob realized that he wasn't going to be able to get on with his work for a while so he sat down at the computer terminal and faced Luke. "Not all my medical file has disappeared, then. Yeah, it was leukaemia."

"Not nice."

Bob grunted. "It chewed me up and spat me out. That's how it made me feel. Crushed. If you think I look a bit scrawny now, you should've seen me then. I didn't feel human at all. I was a mockery of a man. I did every drug, every antibiotic, I had my blood replaced I don't know how many times, and then there was radiotherapy. I leaked watery blood at every opportunity and got every infection going. My joints ached all the time and I bruised incredibly easily. I was amazingly weak. Near death, they said." He shook his head at the memory. "Leukaemia bruises the spirit as well, you know. One minute I was desperate to carry on living and the next I was desperate to die. I guess I wanted to end the torment one way or another. I wanted a life worth something or the comfort of death."

"I suppose that means you believe in euthanasia."

"Well. . ." He paused before making up his mind and

continuing. "It's tricky, isn't it? I might've opted for it at one stage but. . ." He spread his arms. "Here I am. A survivor, thanks to a successful bone-marrow transplant. You don't switch someone's life support off if there's even a remote chance they're going to pull round."

"True." But Luke was thinking of patients who would never pull round because they had a terminal condition. He shrugged and changed the subject. "Do you like chocolate?"

"You've got to be kidding! Everyone thinks this is a dream job, but the ones who come to work here because they love the stuff soon get sick of the sight of it."

Luke laughed. "I guess, if you get biscuits – or make your own – they wouldn't be chocolate ones."

"Definitely not."

"Do you make your own, then?" Luke asked.

"No." Apparently more eager to talk about his work, Bob asked, "Do you know how much chocolate this country gets through every year? Three hundred million kilograms."

At once, Malc corrected him. "Three hundred and twenty-five million kilograms, which equates to thirteen kilograms per person per year on average."

Smiling, Luke said, "Malc could probably tell us quite a lot about chocolate."

"It is prepared from ground roasted cocoa beans and usually sweetened. It is a rich source of energy and also contains small amounts of the stimulants, theobromine and caffeine. The beans come from the tropical cacao tree, *Theobroma cacao*—"

Luke interrupted. "Okay. Thanks, Malc."

Throughout the interview, Luke was aware that Bob Beckham fitted Nyree's description of the Heather Man. His hair was a curious mixture of almost black and an old man's grey. Perhaps his cancer had taken its toll, ageing him prematurely. The stubble on his cheeks and chin was also dark and silvery in patches.

"The other day," Luke said, "I was talking to Sandy Chipperfield and Julian Bent about you."

Bob looked bewildered. "Who?"

"Never mind. It doesn't matter. You must have a lot of sympathy with people in hospital."

"Of course."

"Are you the one they call the Heather Man?"

Again, Bob took a moment to reply. "I didn't know that's what they call me but, yes, I give heather to people who look like they need some luck."

"Julian Bent didn't want your flowers but you dropped a bit when you went in to see him."

"Did I?" Bob replied. "I don't take names in, I'm afraid."

"You gave a bunch to Sandy Chipperfield. It was a nice idea, but. . ."

"She didn't make it?"

Luke shook his head.

"I'm sorry to hear that."

"Did you give her anything else?" said Luke.

Puzzled, Bob frowned. "No. I just do my bit with lucky heather."

"Okay. Thanks," Luke replied. "You've been very helpful." At the door, he turned back and said, "The other day, a friend of mine gave me some chocolate made with castor beans. Would that be any good, do you reckon?"

Bob shrugged. "Never heard of it. At least it'd make a change."

Luke smiled. "Yeah. I guess so. Does this factory import castor beans as well as cocoa?"

"I don't know. As I said, I've never heard of it."

Walking away from the factory, Luke asked Malc, "Now you've seen Bob Beckham – the Heather Man – he wasn't one of the Visionaries, was he?"

"No."

"Log on to the chocolate company's computer, Malc. Is there any record of them importing castor beans or castor-oil plants?"

Malc worked on the remote access for six minutes. "There is no such record."

"Like there's no record of Beckham's bone-marrow transplant."

"You seem to be implying something without stating it clearly."

"Come on! Bob Beckham works on computers. He could've deleted a few things from his medical files and got rid of any record of him adding castor beans to one of the factory's cocoa consignments."

"Speculation."

"I'll speculate, you concentrate on his blood sample. And that's another thing. When I told him I was taking a thumb prick, his face fell."

"Incorrect. Also, it is impossible unless he has also had a face transplant and rejected the foreign tissue."

Luke opened his mouth but, for a few seconds, words failed him.

Malc announced, "I have a request for sound-only communication from the chief pathologist."

"Good." Apparently talking to the air, Luke said, "Forensic Investigator Luke Harding here."

"You ordered an analysis of Charlie Illingworth's stomach contents."

"Yes."

"Well, most of his nutrition was delivered by tube. The stomach didn't contain very much at all. Most of the little that he did eat had already been digested. But I did find some traces adhering to his mucosal folds."

"What was it?"

The pathologist answered, "In this game, it's mainly a matter of visual inspection. They're oats and chewed seed cases. The sort of thing you get in flapjacks."

Luke smiled. "Exactly what I wanted to know. Can you do a full analysis on the bits of seed cases? I think I can guess, but that's not good enough. I've got to be sure what sort of seeds they are."

"I'll do it as soon as I can and report back."

"Thanks," Luke said. After Malc broke the connection, he added, "This case is steaming all of a sudden. I reckon I've got another murder by ricin. What I need now is a link between a suspect and a supply of castor beans. And the motive."

Chapter Twenty-One

The sun had gone down. Luke was staring out of his hotel window at the glittering lights of York, thinking of his sister. He was too young at the time to remember the dreadful splodge on the right-hand side of her brain scan. He was too young to remember Kerryanne throwing back painkillers that helped her a little and throwing up anti-nausea pills that didn't help at all. The doctors' increasingly desperate treatments gave her a few extra months of life — sort-of life anyway — before that final night under the stars with her parents and big brother.

To Luke's sore eyes, the city lights were fuzzy. And they appeared to sway slightly. When Malc began to speak and Luke turned his head, dizziness and daggers seemed to attack his brain. But at least Malc had good news.

"Jade Vernon is requesting a link."

"Put her on the telescreen."

"Hiya!" she said before hesitating and adding, "You look pale."

"Pyramids don't work right away," Luke replied with a pained grin.

"Maybe it'll take a day or two."

"Mmm. If a pain goes away on its own after you've tried some crazy remedy, it gets the credit even though it hasn't done anything."

"As long as you get better, it doesn't matter. Is Malc looking after you?"

"Well? Are you?" Luke asked his mobile.

"I continue to monitor your health. For example, I am bouncing an invisible laser beam off your upper body to calculate your respiration rate from chest vibrations."

Jade said to Luke, "Bombarded by a laser, eh? No wonder you're feeling off."

Malc answered, "I am utilizing a beam that has no ill effects on humans."

"I'm doing my bit as well," said Jade. "Trying to make you feel better. I'm working on a new song, just for you. Something with words. Not many. Just a simple message. It'll be about looking at the stars. It's going to be full of space. Sad but soothing. Listen."

She picked up an acoustic guitar and strummed the first few chords. They echoed with a touching emptiness.

"Perfect," said Luke.

"Early days," she replied. "The first verse goes something like: *They make the sweetest sound, just for a moment, then they're gone.* After that. . . I don't know. But I'm on the job."

"Thanks. Sounds terrific."

Bringing Luke back down to earth, Malc announced, "I have completed the analysis of the blood sample taken from the suspect at York Chocolate Factory."

Jade laughed. "Don't let me keep you from a good

blood sample."

"Sorry, Jade, but it's important. Not that your song isn't. . ."

"It's all right, forensic investigator. Back to work for both of us. Take care."

Once the image on the large screen had faded, Malc said, "Blood from Bob Beckham and Peter Sachs is identical."

Luke fisted the air. "Yes! A new song and a good result."

"It confirms that Peter Sachs was the source of Bob Beckham's bone marrow. Bob Beckham has admitted that he is the Heather Man so it is likely that his hospital visits account for the DNA traces left near several patients. The finding does not prove that he has committed a crime."

"Agreed. Giving bunches of flowers isn't against the law, is it?"

"No."

"But did he give them anything more than heather?"

"Unknown."

"I bet you're going to tell me it doesn't prove my father's innocent either."

"There is now no convincing evidence that Dr Sachs saw the victims, but his innocence or guilt has yet to be established."

"But the motive's got nothing to do with alternative medicine."

"Correct. He has a different reason to kill. Dr Sachs has the medical knowledge to assist or enforce suicide to end suffering. He stated that he is in favour of euthanasia under some circumstances. Also, when he was talking to you about his daughter, he said, 'She died with dignity.' I conclude that this suspect believes that people have a right to die with dignity. In fact, The Authorities have never recognized any such right in law."

Luke nodded, trying not to think about whether his sister died naturally or at the hands of a kind-hearted father. "Yeah. I know. But Beckham's the prime suspect now. It makes sense if he's a mercy killer because we know the Heather Man doesn't go into the Children's Ward much. That's because old people are much more likely to have fatal diseases. I know Beckham said euthanasia worried him, but he would say that if he's guilty." Luke thought about it and then laughed to himself. "Bob's got the same DNA as my father, making him a sort of twin brother. So, when Father said, 'Bob's your uncle,' to me, he was very nearly right."

"The identical DNA was not an accident of nature. Therefore, the chief suspect cannot be your uncle."

"No. It was a joke."

Malc replied, "A prefrontal-cortex region of the human brain is necessary to understand a joke. I do not possess such an organ."

"Pity. Anyway, the Institute of Biomechanical Research

is second on my list, with the motive of harvesting human bodies. Have you detected anything that links Oscar Hislop – or any of the research staff – to castor beans?"

"No."

"I'd better go and look tomorrow, then. And you'd better send a message to the Brain Injury Unit because Hislop's been there. Get the ward supervisor to check if any of her patients have been given biscuits. If they have, tell her to confiscate them – and keep them somewhere safe."

"Transmitting." Malc hesitated before adding, "You may be interested to know that Oscar Hislop is currently working a late shift at the Institute of Biomechanical Research."

Luke groaned. "You want me to rush around with a head like a lead weight, absolutely knackered."

"According to my dictionary, a knacker is someone who slaughters worn-out horses for use as animal food or fertiliser. It can also mean a person who acquires old buildings or ships to reuse their constituent materials."

"Knackered means too exhausted to make a new entry in your dictionary."

"It requires no effort on your behalf. I can log the new definition."

"Go on, then." Luke reached for his coat. "I may be knackered but it's too good an opportunity to miss. Come on. I'm going back to the hospital."

Beyond the reception and twenty-four-hour snack bar, the large building had become quiet and faintly sinister after normal visiting hours. Now and again, a member of staff strolled along a passageway, a door slid open or shut, a cleaner mopped a floor with dilute disinfectant, someone was wheeled from one place to another on a trolley, and late-night drinks were delivered to the wards. Otherwise, it was as calm as a crematorium. Most of the patients were sleeping peacefully or fitfully next to monitors that occasionally emitted high-pitched beeps.

Surprised to see a visitor so late in the evening, Oscar Hislop looked away from the machine that was slowly increasing the tension applied to one of CI's deformed bones, bending it like an archer's bow. "Again?" he said.

Luke nodded. "It's not very important but you might be able to help me."

Oscar studied Luke's face for a moment, perhaps not believing him. "You're young for an FI. How old are you?"

"Sixteen."

His lips formed a twisted smile. "A bit older than me."

"Sorry?"

"Most adults can claim to be fifteen years old on average."

"What?"

"Fifteen's the average age of the cells inside us all." Eager to show off, Oscar explained, "You see, a sixty-year-old's skin is only two weeks old because the body

167

sheds the worn-out stuff and remakes a nice new layer every couple of weeks or so. That's what a lot of dust is: dead skin. A sixty-year-old's brain is sixty years old, though, because the brain doesn't regenerate nerve cells. At the other extreme, the lining of the gut takes a real hammering and gets renewed every five days. Even people's bones are replaced every ten years. So, our bodies are always in a state of breakdown and regeneration. On average, they're a lot younger than we are. Good, eh? You'll get through quite a few bodies before you die. Unless you die soon."

Was that supposed to be good-humoured banter or a threat? Luke wasn't sure. He ignored the comment. "So, next time someone asks how old I am, I should say, 'Which bit are you talking about?'"

Oscar grinned at him. "Exactly."

Under the protective plastic plate, Charlie's bone snapped and the computer took a reading of the force required to break it.

Luke asked, "Do you ever do any experiments with ricin?"

"Ricin? That's chemistry, not mechanics. No, nothing to do with the institute." He nodded towards Charlie Illingworth's broken bone. "We're all about physical forces on the body and how organs behave under stress."

"Obviously, you know what ricin is, though."

"It's famous," Oscar replied. "Infamous, really. So, yes,

I've heard of it. But I've never worked with it. I wouldn't want to, either, from what I've heard. If you're interested, go and see the Poisoning Unit. Or Peter Sachs in the Department of Alternative Medicine. That's his kettle of fish — biologically active chemicals in plants."

Luke tried not to react to the reference to his father. "Okay. But do you know which plant it comes from?"

"No. Doesn't your machine know these things?" He paused and then said, "Of course it does. You're testing me."

"You get it from castor beans, seeds of the castor-oil plant."

Oscar shrugged. "News to me."

"So, when I search these labs, your computer, and all your staff's living quarters, including yours, I won't find any?"

"I can't vouch for everyone but I wouldn't have thought so. Certainly nothing to do with work, that's for sure."

"What about biscuits?"

"What about them?"

"Do you have any?"

"Yeah. Lots," Oscar replied. "Love them. We keep a big plastic container topped up with them. The more chocolate, the better."

"I'll take a look, please. And you'd better download a list of all your colleagues into my mobile."

"What is this?" Oscar said. "What do you think we've done? Is it. . .? Oh, I see. You think we're poisoning patients to order."

"It crossed my mind," Luke admitted.

"Not true," Oscar replied.

"How do I know that?"

"Because I told you. Because we're decent and kind. We're not a rogue outfit."

Chapter Twenty-Two

The next morning, Malc rattled off his latest batch of information. "The ward supervisor of the Brain Injury Unit has reported that none of the patients has been given biscuits or heather. There have not been any deaths overnight. Agents have searched the Institute of Biomechanical Research and its staff's living quarters. There was no evidence of castor-oil plants or their seeds."

"All right. That means one of two things. Either Oscar Hislop and his workmates haven't been harvesting human specimens, or they have and they're very careful." Luke hesitated, thinking about it. "They're research scientists. I bet they know every forensic method we've got. That means they'd know how to cover their tracks."

"In the absence of evidence, that is speculation."

"Yeah." Luke grabbed his coat and headed for the front door. "I want to check out a different lead. Well, I don't want to, but I haven't got much choice. Come on. Back to Malton."

By the time that he reached his parents' home through pouring rain, they had both left for work. His forensic investigator's identity card granted him access to their cottage but he felt ashamed to intrude without their knowledge or permission. He would have preferred to act like a son, not like an investigator.

Wiping his feet thoroughly on the mat so that he did not leave a watery trail on the flooring, he stepped inside and closed the door. Trying to ignore the feeling that he was somehow a traitor, he said, "Right. Where do we start? In the kitchen, I suppose."

Luke pulled on a pair of latex gloves. Starting on the right-hand side, he went through every cupboard while Malc recorded and logged each find. It didn't take long to discover jars of flour, oats and desiccated coconut. He also found a packet of linseed in the tiled pantry, along with his father's juice with a kick. Luke unscrewed the top of the bottle and sniffed it. Curious, he held it out towards Malc. "What's this?"

Malc analysed the fumes in a matter of seconds. "The drink contains a moderately high content of ethanol, known mostly as intoxicating alcohol. It is used to depress the central nervous system. It relaxes inhibitions, eases tensions, and impairs judgement."

Luke tightened the cap and put the bottle back. "So, it'd help to forget a painful past."

"Temporarily, yes."

Luke nodded and continued his search. When he'd finished his circuit of the kitchen, he sighed. "Well, I've got all the ingredients for those biscuits, except the most important one. Castor beans."

"There's a greenhouse at the rear of the property," Malc reminded him.

"Ah, yes. I remember walking past it." Luke was not expecting his mother or father to return for hours so he made for the back door. With a heavy heart, he pulled his waterproof hood over his head and made a dash for the greenhouse.

Luke recognized the potted bushes either side of the door. He'd tended the same plants for a while at Birmingham School. And he'd stolen their heavy fruit as often as he thought that he could get away with it. The fresh juicy pomegranates were worth the risk. Luke shivered as a cold trickle of water ran down his neck. Pelting the panes of glass, the rain sounded worse than it really was outside. Sluicing the windows, it blurred the view.

The large greenhouse was providing a harbour for sensitive plants over winter. On the sturdy benches down both sides, there were numerous potted plants. Some, like a big tray of cacti, were grown merely for show. Others would provide crops later in the year. Apart from the small pomegranate trees, Luke did not recognize individual species, but Malc hovered at his shoulder, photographing and identifying each plant by comparison with his wildlife database.

Half way down the aisle, the mobile came to an abrupt halt beside two particular pots.

Anticipating Malc's devastating announcement, Luke slumped against the rough wooden bench with his head in his hands.

173

Chapter Twenty-Three

Malc's discovery of two castor-oil plants in the greenhouse was followed by a long, uncomfortable silence. Luke didn't need the time to work out what the finding meant. It was obvious. He needed the time to come to terms with the damning evidence against his father.

It was Malc who cut through the silence. "It is unusual that a suspect of Dr Sachs's intelligence would leave a murder weapon clearly visible in such an incriminating location."

Luke looked up at his mobile. At once, he saw a chance that his father was innocent, despite the blatant evidence. "Yes. Of course! You're right. It's a plant!"

"That is beyond doubt," Malc replied. "It is *Ricinus communis*."

"No," Luke snapped. This time, he was unable to see the funny side of Malc's limited vocabulary. "I mean it's been put here deliberately to make Father look guilty."

"Unproven."

Fired up, Luke looked around. He needed to find evidence that someone else had brought the castor-oil plants into the greenhouse. Beneath his feet were flagstones. There were no clear shoeprints on them. The only marks were the dribbles from his own shoes and they would soon dry to nothing. The only surfaces capable of holding a fingerprint were the glass panes of the greenhouse itself and the plastic tubs. "Scan these two pots for prints, Malc."

"There is none."

"That's weird," Luke replied. "And suspicious."

"Not necessarily. The person handling them may have worn gardening gloves."

Luke pulled a face. "I'd put gloves on to touch a spiky cactus or something filthy, but not these. If they were Father's, they'd have his prints. Surely."

"You are required to conduct all investigations without bias," Malc warned him.

"Yeah, all right. I know. A lack of prints isn't enough to prove someone else put them here."

Luke walked up and down the gangway between the two benches as rain cascaded down the glass.

"The soil, Malc! I want an analysis of the soil in all these pots. If they're all the same, apart from the castor-oil plants, they probably came from somewhere else."

"That is a logical approach," said Malc. "I will begin with an examination of microscopic quartz grains to identify the source of each earth sample. If the pots contain compost, chemical analysis will be required to identify different types."

"Sounds like a long job."

"I cannot provide an estimate until the amount of

testing required becomes clear."

"All right. Get started anyway. Look," said Luke, pointing underneath the bench. "There's a big bag of compost. I'll drag it out so you can compare it with what's in the plant pots."

"Task logged. My access to the soil would be improved if you took a small sample out of each container and laid them in order on the concrete floor."

"Anything to speed it up."

Still wearing the latex gloves, Luke began by moving a pot containing a palm with long red and rough leaves. He set it down on a paving stone and then straightened up, looking for a small trowel. But he hesitated when he saw the part of the bench where the palm had stood. The outline of the bottom of the pot was marked neatly by scattered and spilt soil. Inside the circle, the wooden surface was clean.

Straight away, Luke moved one of the cacti and found exactly the same effect. "Take a visual record of this, Malc," he said, pointing to the ring of dirt that defined the shape of the pot. "See?"

"The plants were arranged on a clean surface some time ago," Malc deduced. "Wind has since blown soil particles around each base, creating an outline."

"So," Luke said with a desperate smile, "if these castor-oil plants have been here for a long time, they'll be the same."

"That is valid reasoning."

"Right then." His heartbeat accelerated as he took hold of the first castor-oil plant and lifted it up in its container.

Underneath, the shape of the pot was not marked by soil and the bench was not clean. The plant had been put down on a thin layer of dirt.

"This specimen is not as established as the others," Malc observed.

"You mean, it's just been dumped here. Recently. It hasn't sat here over winter."

"Confirmed."

Luke put it down and tried the second castor-oil plant. Like the first, it was a recent addition to the greenhouse. "I bet someone put it here last night, trying to frame my father. So," Luke said, "who knew Peter Sachs was in the firing line?" Luke did not have to think very hard to answer his own question. "His DNA twin. Bob Beckham."

"You should note that Oscar Hislop also referred to Peter Sachs last night. His comment could be interpreted as an accusation."

"He could've backed it up with this plant."

"Speculation. Your father or mother could have simply moved these two pots recently."

"Scrap the soil analysis for now. We're going inside. I want a telescreen link to Peter Sachs."

In the living room, the close-up of Peter's face expressed bewilderment. "You're at home? My home? In

177

Malton?"

"Sorry, but I had to check out your greenhouse. Malc's going to split your screen so you can see a plant. I want you to tell me if you recognize it as one of yours."

Luke watched as his father's eyes focused to one side for a few seconds. Then he lifted a tumbler to his lips and took a drink.

"Yeah, well. It's not mine. I think. . . I'm not sure. . ." He examined the image again. "Yes. I know. It's your mother's. She got two of them last autumn. Maybe September. I didn't know where she put them. Anyway, she keeps moving them around."

Luke was stunned.

"Luke? What have I said?"

It was Malc who filled the silence. "You have stated that Elisa Harding—"

"Shut up, Malc!" Luke said. Talking to his father, Luke asked, "Are you sure about that?"

"I think so. Your mother tells me I forget things but. . ." He shrugged. "Why?"

"Does she ever turn up at the hospital?"

"She's in good shape."

"That's not what I mean. Does she visit?"

"Well, I've never bumped into her and she hasn't said anything about it. If she did, she would've dropped in on me, I would've thought. What's on your mind? What's going on?"

"I don't know," Luke replied, stretching the truth. "I've got to go, but I'll let you know as soon as I sort it out."

Malc terminated the link before Peter could ask anything else.

Luke took a deep breath and muttered, "Mother!"

Coldly, Malc said, "Elisa Harding called herself a silly emotional astronomer. You should consider the possibility that the death of her daughter disturbed the balance of her mind."

That was exactly what Luke was doing. He was wondering if his mother didn't want anyone else to suffer in the same way as Kerryanne. He was wondering if she was providing a way out for people with intolerable lives. But a motive and a weapon didn't make her guilty. To be a serious suspect, she had to have the opportunity as well. Could she really have taken biscuits laced with castor beans to the hospital on at least twenty occasions? Could she really slip away from her job so often? Or would she have done it out of working hours? Could she have fed poisoned biscuits to Charlie Illingworth and Sandy Chipperfield? If Julian Bent didn't need help to eat, would she have left him with a biscuit to chew and swallow when he was ready?

"Malc. Priority jobs. Send Elisa Harding's picture to the ward supervisors of the three known victims and to Sandy's and Julian's partners. Get them to tell you if they recognize her. Log on to the North York Moors

Observatory's computer and look for files on staff attendance. Can you do that? Has Mother. . . has Elisa Harding been absent a lot in the past six months?"

"Processing tasks."

Luke sat back and closed his eyes. He dreaded the answers.

Chapter Twenty-Four

Luke went to the back door where he'd hung his coat. Underneath it were two little puddles. He wiped them up with a kitchen towel before slipping the sodden coat back on and leaving. He was speeding towards his hotel in York, still locked in his depressing thoughts, when Malc started to deliver results. "The pathologist at York Hospital has confirmed that some of the seed-case fragments in Charlie Illingworth's stomach were from castor beans. The staff database at the observatory in Fylingdales has not recorded frequent absences by Elisa Harding. Sandy Chipperfield's partner, Marvin, does not recognize the image of your latest suspect. I await three other responses."

"Is my mother at work now?"

"Confirmed."

"Good." Luke knew that he would have to interview her but he hated the idea.

"Do you want me to establish a connection?"

"Not yet," Luke replied. "I want those other answers first — and a telescreen."

He did not have long to prepare himself. Within half an hour, Malc announced that none of the three supervisors recognized Elisa as a visitor to their wards. Finally, Romilly Dando reported in. She could not be certain, but she did not recall anyone matching Elisa's description near her partner's room at the hospital.

At least that was a relief. But it was a long way from proving Elisa Harding's innocence. Back in his hotel room, Luke sighed and sat down opposite the telescreen. "All right, Malc. Time for that link to the observatory."

His mother's smiling face decorated the wall. "Good to hear from you again," she said. "Are you all right? No more cuts and bruises?"

"I'm fine. I was just wondering what you're doing right now."

"Me? I'm doing what I always do, Luke. One of three things. I get ready to look up at the stars, I look up at the stars, and I study data from the last time I. . . you guessed it. Right now, I'm working on information collected in the last few weeks. I'm watching a star die on my monitor. It's. . . awesome and sad. Really moving."

Luke nodded. "I can imagine."

"Are you sure you're all right?"

"I just want you to take a look at a plant in your greenhouse. Malc will put a picture of it on your screen. Okay?"

Elisa paused for a few seconds. "Yes. It's in front of me now." A moment later, she looked back at Luke. "I don't know why you're interested but I've never seen it before."

"Really? But Father said. . ."

"Oh, your father! Don't believe what he says. Sozzled

half the time. Wouldn't know a pomegranate tree if it fell on him."

"But he said it was yours."

"He's wrong."

"Did you order a couple of new plants last autumn?"

"Yes. Maybe, if someone'd drunk a lot, they'd mistake them for what you've got there but. . . no. They're not the ones. They're not mine. I don't know where they've come from."

Murderers almost always denied owning the weapon. That was nothing new. But this denial was different. It came from his own mother and Luke wanted to believe it. "Have you come across stone-man syndrome?"

His mother frowned. "Sounds strange. I don't think so."

But Luke saw a flicker of recognition in her face. "Sure?"

"Well, now you mention it, maybe I have. Maybe Peter's said something about it, but. . . I don't know. Luke, this is feeling more and more like an interrogation. What's going on?"

"Bear with me. I'm checking something out for the hospital."

"And your father's involved, is he? He's upset, you know. Been upset for eleven years. And the drinking doesn't help."

"What do you think about euthanasia?"

With a mischievous grin, she said, "Your father's not that far gone. I'm not ready to have him put down yet."

"No, I mean, what's your stance on it? In general."

"Peter's all for it, but not me. Never. Not after our experience with Kerryanne. I had to give her every possible moment, every chance of life."

"I don't suppose Father would have. . . no."

Elisa did not look as shocked as she should have been. "I know what you're saying, Luke. I've thought about it myself. But, no. He wouldn't have done anything to shorten her life. It was cancer that caught up with your sister. Her time had come, like this star on my computer. As simple and heartbreaking – and natural – as that. Believe me. I would've known if there'd been any funny business."

After his mother's face disappeared from the telescreen, Luke stood up and touched his stomach. "Something in here tells me Bob Beckham's still at the top of the list."

"In that region of the human body, there are no organs that are capable of providing insight."

"It's called instinct."

"It is not admissible in law," the mobile replied.

"Well, maybe I feel like that because of the gaps in Beckham's hospital record. The missing bits are too convenient to be a simple mistake. It smells like deliberate tinkering to blame a transplant donor." After a moment's hesitation, he added, "Don't take the smell too literally."

"The transplant procedure is carried out anonymously. The recipient would not have known that the bone marrow came from Dr Sachs."

"He's a computer engineer, Malc! He hacked in and got the information. Then he deleted it to cover his tracks."

"I am receiving a high-priority message from the Spinal Injury Section in York."

"What is it?"

"A patient is claiming that he was fed a biscuit to help end his life. He has since changed his mind."

Once more, Luke grabbed his coat. "Okay. The quickest way is to run."

Luke hurtled down the passageway, swerving round patients, staff and visitors, before crashing into the Spinal Injury Section. "Forensic Investigator Harding," he yelled at the first nurse that he saw.

"Room 4," she said, pointing him in the right direction.

He dashed into the cubicle which was the focus of frantic activity by two doctors from the poisoning unit and two nurses. There were tubes everywhere and several bowls of foul-smelling fluids. "Ricin," Luke announced. "That's what was in the biscuit. Castor beans."

One of the doctors looked up from the patient. "Are you sure?"

"Certain."

"Another gastric flush, nurse."

"I've already—"

"Again!" He yelled at the second nurse, "Get me magnesium trisilicate. Lots of it. What the flush doesn't bring up, I'll absorb with that. Quickly."

"Can I talk to him?" Luke asked.

"Yeah," the second doctor replied with sarcasm. "We've only got two tubes down his throat."

The patient was still conscious, though. He was lying on his side, staring helplessly at the wall like an uncomprehending child or a sick animal. Luke said to his mobile, "Project an image onto this wall, Malc. Elisa Harding."

Luke looked down at the patient's face. He seemed to be looking at Elisa's photograph but there was no sign of recognition in his eyes.

Next, Luke tried a picture of Bob Beckham. Then Peter Sachs and Oscar Hislop.

None of the images drew a response from the sick man. Maybe he was gazing at something beyond the wall. Maybe he didn't understand the point. Maybe he was beyond caring.

Luke sighed and withdrew, comforted at least by the thought that, if the doctors saved the man's life, he'd be an eyewitness. If he lived, Luke might have an easy way of concluding the case.

On his way out of the treatment room, Luke noticed a

sprig of heather pinned to the door.

The air was damp with mist but it had stopped raining. Identity card in hand, Luke hesitated outside York Chocolate Factory and took a deep breath. "All right," he muttered. "I'm ready."

"Your respiration rate is well above normal," Malc noted. "Also, I detect some sweating."

"Well, I'm sorry I'm not as cool as you when I'm trying to trap the chief suspect. Come on."

The manager who escorted Luke to the common room where Bob Beckham was taking a coffee break said over her shoulder, "He's not in trouble, is he?"

"I don't know," Luke answered. "I just want to talk to him."

"He's got a knack with computers. We'd be lost without him." She paused by a door that slid open automatically. "Here we go. Do you know him by sight or. . .?"

Luke nodded. "Yes. I can see him. Thanks. I'll take it from here."

Surprised by Luke's unannounced arrival, Bob stood up, holding his mug in both hands.

Almost everyone in the room was wearing blue overalls with the company's logo on the front. Walking past a group of workers who were laughing loudly, Luke went straight up to Beckham. Shaking his head, Luke said,

"Big mistake. The spinal-injury patient. He ate the biscuit but changed his mind. The doctors saved him. He's an eyewitness now."

Luke expected to provoke an instant reaction but didn't anticipate what it would be.

Bob's hand jerked and Luke felt the sting of hot coffee on his face. The assault was so sudden and violent that not even Malc was quick enough to prevent it. The laughter behind them ceased abruptly as Luke cried out and clamped his hands to his face, still bearing its stitched gash.

Bob shouldered his way through the crowd of workers and sprinted to the door.

Malc could not get a clear shot at the suspect because of the other staff taking a break. Besides, he had not been ordered to fire.

Luke used his fingers to wipe the coffee away from his smarting eyes and from the cut that was stinging unpleasantly. "I'm all right," he said, blinking over and over again. "Come on! Pursuit and defence mode. Don't harm him. He hasn't admitted anything yet."

The group of startled workers parted to let Luke through. The door sprang back, revealing a large circular tank. Several paddles attached to a central spindle stirred thick brown sludge and pushed it out into a channel like a waterway. Bob Beckham had clambered over the chute and was squeezing through a gap in the mechanism.

Luke would have been confident of catching the fleeing suspect if he'd been feeling fit. He would have been very confident of Malc catching Beckham if he hadn't just disappeared through an opening that was too narrow for a Mobile Aid to Law and Crime to pass through.

Luke dashed across the arena, vaulted athletically over the river of chocolate and peered through the gap. He couldn't see where Bob had gone and he couldn't hear his footsteps because of the churning machines. Next to Luke, an overpowering smell came from the liquid chocolate as it oozed over the edge. Underneath, the sickly cascade filled one mould after another. Somewhere down there, Bob Beckham was getting away.

Luke squeezed through the same gap and clambered onto a stainless-steel ladder. "You find another way down to the next level," he said to Malc.

"I must protect—"

"If you can't catch up with me, go outside and patrol the building. Don't let him get away, but use minimum force."

Ignoring his mobile's protests, Luke descended the steps.

He found himself on a metal platform, positioned above another vat. This time the liquid chocolate below him was milky white. He peered over the rail, trying to spot the computer engineer. There were quite a few people in the company's overalls attending the production line, but none of them looked like Beckham.

Luke realized too late that someone was behind him. Before he could react, he felt the force of two hands on his back. The push tipped him over the handrail and he fell.

Chapter Twenty-Five

He wheeled once in the air and plunged head-first into the vast barrel of chocolate. He tried to cry out when his left leg hit one of the rotating paddles but, submerged in the sweet tacky fluid, the shriek died on his lips.

It was nothing like water. It was nothing like swimming. The warm gummy emulsion coated him heavily, dragging him down like quicksand. In water, he could have released his breath in a burst of bubbles but here the goo pressed densely against his mouth like a gag. His ears were clogged with the stuff so he could hear absolutely nothing. His eyes clamped shut. Neither his hands nor feet could touch the bottom of the tank as the paddle shoved him slowly round.

Frantically, he thrust out his arms, trying to spin himself around before he lost consciousness. It was like trying to manoeuvre in glue but he managed to make a quarter turn. The metal plate that had been pushing against his back now pressed into his side. Really, he wanted to face the paddle. He flapped his arms again, attempting to twist further round. He became so disorientated in that silent, sightless swirl that he was no longer certain which way was up and which was down.

Seconds seemed like minutes. His mouth opened and filled with suffocating chocolate. His chest seemed to be about to burst. He made one final effort to spin round, fighting the flow of the sticky fluid. He managed to hook his right elbow around the revolving blade. That gave him the leverage he needed. With the paddle now forced against his chest, he could place both hands on it. Taking a moment to work out his orientation, he propelled himself upward to where the chocolate seemed thinner.

His head broke the surface just as his lungs exploded. White globules spurted from his mouth and nose. Then he gasped down a mixture of air and chocolate. Clinging doggedly to the paddle that had now stopped turning, he coughed again and again, scattering more of the horrible stuff.

A couple of people in blue overalls and hairnets held out their hands, grabbed him under the arms and tugged him out of the cloying sludge, like a powerless seabird daubed with oily pollution.

Luke collapsed against the side of the vat, his fingers rubbing around his eyes, still wheezing and coughing repeatedly.

The horrified workers who had turned off the mechanism gathered around him with the same question. "Are you all right?"

Luke dragged his fingers through his long heavy hair and found it blended with chocolate. "I'm. . . okay. Did you. . .?" He gulped down more air before he could finish his question. "Did you see Bob Beckham?"

Someone answered, "He went towards Packaging." She pointed to a door that led down to another level towards the back of the building.

"Thanks," Luke said. He tried to run towards the door but it was more like a stagger. His feet were encased in chocolate, his left leg was badly bruised and his coat dripped white slush.

One of the staff called after him, "You've had a shock. You shouldn't. . ."

But the advice went unheard. Luke was oblivious to the commotion behind him.

Spluttering, he lurched down a ramp onto the next floor and followed a long conveyor belt carrying wrapped chocolate bars towards another machine. On the other side of it, large boxes of packaged product emerged. One after another, they trundled along on rollers until they reached a stacking stage.

Here, they were within range of forklift trucks and a crane. One crate had just been loaded onto auto-barge 0147 and the vessel was now steering out into the centre of the canal, ready to make its journey to a supplier. And that's when Luke caught sight of the leg of a blue overall.

He dashed towards the only supervisor that he could see. Pulling his identity card out of a chocolatey pocket, he waved it in front of the bemused woman. "Do you have people on the auto-barges?"

"Er. . . no. They're automatic." She was too dazed by

Luke's appearance to say any more. She just stared at him.

"That's it, then," Luke muttered to himself. Again, a suspect was getting away from him on a boat. "Where's Malc?"

In the cold air, the chocolate was solidifying on his clothing and in his hair. Some of it began to crack and fall away from him in small jagged pieces while he scampered back around the factory. As he stumbled on, he barely noticed the glasshouse where all sorts of exotic ornamental plants were growing.

He found his mobile at the front of the factory, about to begin a circuit of the building.

"You're too late," Luke told him, screwing a little finger into his ear to dig out hardened, white-chocolate-like wax. At once, his hearing improved. "Beckham's on a barge, heading north. I want you to plot me a route by fast cab to a bridge over the canal and I want to get there before the boat."

Malc was not surprised by Luke's bizarre appearance because he was never surprised. "Consulting maps and calculating."

Luke walked up and down impatiently for two minutes, picking chocolate from his hair, face and fingernails.

"Task complete. A cab will be here within a minute."

"Where am I going?"

"To Tollerton. The freeway crosses the canal there.

Using the average speed of an electric cab and an auto-barge, you will reach the bridge seven minutes and thirty-three seconds before the boat."

"Good. Time to make myself feel less like a walking soft-centre."

Luke was gripping the handrail of the bridge with both arms as he stood perilously on the narrow ledge above the canal. Remaining on the safe side of the barrier, Malc said, "I caution against your intended action. Your health is deteriorating and the drop onto a passing auto-barge is hazardous. It requires considerable skill and judgement. Even then, you may be injured in the fall."

"You work it out for me, then, Malc. Do some fancy calculations and tell me when to jump to give me the best chance of a safe landing – on the boat, not in the water. If I go in the canal, the fish'll make a meal of me. I'm real tasty right now."

A small piece of white chocolate fell from his nostril and an auto-barge came into view, chugging towards him.

"Check it, Malc. Is it boat 0147?"

"Confirmed. It is carrying—"

Luke interrupted. "It's carrying Bob Beckham. That's all that matters. Can't you take control of it remotely? Then I wouldn't have to jump."

"Its computer is not responding to me. I deduce that someone has overridden the mechanism and taken control."

"I wonder who that is," Luke muttered.

"You believe you saw Bob Beckham on board and he is a systems engineer so he is likely to be the saboteur."

"Thanks, Malc," said Luke as the boat approached. "Just work out my best chance."

"Move one metre and eighteen centimetres to the right."

Still clinging to the rail, Luke shuffled along. "Okay?" He felt dizzy and sick.

"Your position should be adequate. I will prompt you to jump onto the top of the control room. That way, the distance you fall will be lessened. The cabin roof has a safety bar around it so, if you roll over, you will have something to grip. There is a small ladder attached to the back of the cabin. This will allow you to climb down to the deck. I cannot brief you further because I have no information on the suspect's precise location."

Luke could now make out the ripples at the prow of the boat. He took a deep breath. "Thanks. Won't be long. Wish me luck."

"I have no concept of luck," Malc replied. "You will jump in twenty seconds. Do not try to leap out from the bridge. You must aim to drop vertically."

Luke looked down, beyond his shoes that poked out over the ledge, and gulped. The water was a long way below him – further than the tub of liquid chocolate had been. The height of the auto-barge would shorten the distance he had to fall but he was going to hit a hard surface. He hoped that his nausea was simply the effect of the chocolate. His heart pounded and his head thumped as always. The tension didn't help.

"Ten seconds," Malc said coolly. Then he began a countdown. "Six, five, four, three, two, one, now."

Luke let go of the handrail and jumped down. He tried to tell himself it was just like leaping feet-first into a swimming pool. But this time he knew that his landing wouldn't be cushioned.

Chapter Twenty-Six

Luke felt a dreadful jolt to his ankles, knees and hips as he clattered onto the wooden surface. He couldn't help crying out in pain. His already-injured left leg felt the impact most. He tumbled over and crashed onto one elbow but, remembering Malc's advice, spread his arms. He didn't topple from the turret because his right hand slammed against the railing and he held on tightly.

For a moment, he didn't attempt to get up. He felt like a rag doll, battered and mistreated. But he didn't experience the unrelenting pain of a broken bone. He could move his white-flecked shoes. Steadying himself by clinging to the handrail, he got back onto his feet and staggered towards the ladder.

He didn't know where Beckham was but he could see Malc keeping watch, perched high on one of the crates towards the stern of the boat. If the Heather Man was inside the control room, he would have seen and heard Luke's daring leap onto the roof. But Bob wasn't waiting for him at the bottom of the ladder so Luke turned round and went down backwards on sore and shaking legs.

The barge was moving smoothly on the still surface of the canal. The gangway around the cargo was as steady as a running track. Only the passing buildings of Tollerton and a slight vibration told Luke that he was on board a moving boat.

Luke knew that his mobile had not pinpointed Beckham's whereabouts because he was not coming forward with the information. Malc remained in the position that gave him the best view of the entire cargo boat.

It was tempting to dismiss the idea that Bob was in the control room because he had not come rushing out. But Luke did not turn his back on it straight away. Beckham could be devious enough to stay hidden inside until he could take a retreating Luke by surprise.

Cautiously, Luke opened the door but did not enter. The small room was deserted. The boat's computer had been tugged out of its fitting. Wires bared, it was lying on the console. Next to it, the brass plate was inscribed *Autobarge 0147*. Almost certainly, the vandalized computer was Beckham's work and he'd done it so that a Mobile Aid to Law and Crime could not take control of the barge. Perhaps he was devious. Perhaps he'd anticipated that Luke would catch up with him.

Luke hobbled slowly down one of the gangways, pausing wherever one stack of crates ended and another began. There wasn't much space in between but Bob could well be thin enough to be lurking sideways in any of the gaps. Luke also stopped to examine the fastening on every storage unit because most of them were large enough for a person to stow away inside. A broken lock might mean that Beckham was hidden within. Occasionally, Luke glanced towards Malc to make sure that he was still in the mobile's line of sight. He noticed that the auto-barge had left the village of Tollerton and was heading through the quiet countryside towards Middlesbrough and Sunderland.

At the end of the first gangway – towards the stern – Luke looked up at Malc. "Nothing so far. I'm going back up the other side."

"You should know that, beyond the control room, this vessel has a hatch leading to a secure hold below the main deck."

Luke hesitated. "And what makes it secure?"

"The onboard computer does not allow entry until a code is entered by the legitimate owner at the end of the journey."

"That's the computer Beckham's overridden."

"Correct."

Luke managed to smile. "You know, it doesn't take a genius to work out where he's hiding. You'd better come with me. I think we're going below."

Luke didn't entirely trust his instinct. On the way back to the control room, he still stopped to check out each gap between the crates. But, as he expected, there was nothing. Approaching the prow, he put his head around the corner of the control room. There was no sign of life and the large round hatch was closed.

Almost tiptoeing, Luke walked up to the metal plate with Malc at his side. He knelt down and examined it. A handle in the shape of a steering wheel sealed the door.

"Here goes," Luke whispered.

He took hold of the circular catch with both hands and began to spin it round and round.

"Not much chance of surprising him if he's down here."

After a few seconds, the wheel came to a standstill. Luke adjusted his position and then pulled up the heavy door.

Positioned in the opening, Malc was ready to react to any resistance or assault, but there was nothing to be seen apart from a few steps leading down to a well-lit space. "I will go first," the mobile said.

"Fair enough."

Leaving the hatch open in case he had to make a quick retreat, Luke followed Malc down to the deck below.

A very large container had been lowered into the secure hold before the crates on the main deck had been stacked on top of the access. Now, the only way in and out of the hold was through the hatch. The large storage unit had been forced open and Bob Beckham stood in its fractured doorway.

Holding one arm up at chest height, Bob opened his fist to reveal a handheld electronic device of some sort. "Do you know what this is?"

Luke glanced at his mobile. "Malc?"

"It is the radio-controlled starter for a pyrotechnic display. Before you jumped onto this boat, I attempted to tell you that its cargo includes a large consignment of fireworks."

Bob smiled. "Your robot's right. Someone up north was going to get it. They'd just have to open the crate, arrange the rockets and fountains and all the rest, and press this button. Simple as that. They'd go up in sequence and there'd be a lot of oohs and aahs." Using his free hand, he pointed his thumb over his shoulder at the opened container. "It's a very large display. Someone was planning a very big celebration. That's why it's in the secure hold, I guess. But there won't be any oohing and aahing if I hit the button now. The first firework will set the rest off. That's a lot of explosive detonating at the same time in a confined space."

"Is this right, Malc?"

"Confirmed. Given the number and type of fireworks in the inventory, I calculate that this vessel would be torn apart by the blast. Within ten metres, human life would be exterminated."

"If I can throw coffee in your face before your mobile stops me," Bob said, "I can press this button before it hits me with whatever weapon it's got. And even if I'm wrong, you can't risk me falling on it and setting everything off."

Luke nodded. Turning towards Malc, he said, "Step down from defence mode."

"Status changed."

With a grin, Bob pointed at Luke's head. "Looks like someone's braided your hair with white ribbon."

"Why did you do it, Bob?"

"Why did I push you into the vat of chocolate?"

"You know what I mean. The poisoned biscuits."

He sighed. "Because there comes a stage when there's nothing left but the capacity to feel pain. What's the point of that sort of life?"

"The point is, there's a chance of recovery."

Bob shook his head. "Not with the ones I helped."

"Why did you do it like that – with ricin?"

"Because I believe in nature. I like plants. Some cure people, some bring good luck. When medicine extends your life for no reason, castor beans let you go."

Luke nodded again. "What made you start doing it in the past six months?"

"I didn't," Bob answered. "I've been doing it for years. Ever since my bone-marrow transplant. Keeping the numbers low. But I made a mistake, made it visible to the hospital's statistics. You see, there was a rash of people needing me and I couldn't refuse." Bob paused, plainly thinking about something else. "I'm sorry about Peter Sachs – after what he did for me. He's my blood brother, in a way. But I panicked. I tried to blame him. Will you look him up and tell him I'm sorry?"

"It'd be better if you spoke to him yourself. Why don't you put that controller down and come with me? I could arrange a meeting."

Bob shook his head.

"You're not up for murder, you know. Verify that, Malc."

"Confirmed."

"It'd be a lesser charge. Assisting or maybe enforcing suicide."

"What are you trying to say?"

Luke answered, "That you're not a murderer. You did it with the best of intentions. That'll be taken into account. It's not the death penalty."

"It's years in prison. To me, that's as unbearable as leukaemia."

Ignoring a wave of dizziness and a hammering in his head, Luke took a step towards Bob. "I don't think you'll push that button. You didn't take your life when you were at your worst. You came through it. And, because you're not cruel, you won't kill me."

Bob shook his head. "You're wrong. It's my time. By rights, I should be dead already. I'm not letting you lot give me a terminal condition called a life sentence."

"I'm only an FI," Luke replied. "Sentencing's got nothing to do with me. But maybe it isn't as bad as you think. Maybe just a few years in prison. If you can get through leukaemia, you can get through that."

"I knew the risks. Now, I'm paying the penalty." The controller was lying on his palm and he folded his thumb over until it touched the key.

"No!" Luke cried.

"It's all right," Bob said to him. "I'll give you ten seconds. Did you ever play hide-and-seek when you were a kid? I'll count to ten and you've got that time to go and hide."

Malc stated, "Ten seconds is not sufficient—"

Luke put up his hand to silence his mobile. "I'm not leaving you," he said to Bob. "Come with me and we'll talk to The Authorities. I'll vouch for you. Maybe. . ."

Bob laughed. "No chance. They'll ask if I resisted arrest. They'll ask if I had a go at you. It'll come out that I tried to blame someone else. They won't show me any mercy."

"You just panicked. That's all. It's understandable."

Luke swayed and his vision blurred entirely. He tried to take another step towards Bob but the cargo hold seemed to spin around him. He staggered and groaned. Unable to stop himself, he leaned over and vomited onto the floor.

As soon as FI Luke Harding's life signs dipped outside of the normal range, Malc called silently for medical assistance. Technically, his forensic investigator was too ill to be capable of handling the case so Malc's programming required him to surrender control to The Authorities.

Chapter Twenty-Seven

Bob eyed Luke suspiciously. "You're ill."

Luke's heavy head thumped as if a small angry creature were pounding pitilessly on the inside of his skull. It was even affecting his hearing. The hum of the boat's engine and Bob's voice seemed muffled. He struggled to stand up straight. "Maybe I'm allergic to chocolate," Luke muttered, trying for humour, trying to carry on.

"Big mistake. That's what you said to me. Coming down here was your big mistake." His thumb was still poised above the button on the controller.

"It's not too late," said Luke. "You can still walk away with me. You can do the right thing."

"I know what's right. I'm giving you ten seconds."

"No."

Malc intervened. "Forensic Investigator Harding accepts your proposal."

Astounded, Luke turned towards his mobile. "What?"

"The Authorities require you to leave."

"But. . ."

"This is not a request," Malc said. "It is a command. The life of a forensic investigator takes precedence."

Luke's head spun. The pathetic figure of Bob Beckham appeared to split into two as if he'd generated a twin. Both of the shadowy men seemed to be grasping a remote control for the firework display. Both seemed to be laughing at him. In Luke's mind, they drifted apart and then came back together as a wavering shape like a grotesque clown.

"Ten seconds," someone said.

Something more powerful than Malc or The Authorities told Luke that it was time to go. Intuition. His worsening condition wasn't a hangover from his previous case. It wasn't stress. It wasn't something that would go away of its own accord. Intuition told him that he was dangerously ill. He had to get out.

Luke turned, tottered and made for the steps. Dragging himself up by the handrails on both sides, he made for fresh air.

"Six seconds."

The auto-barge was still cruising peacefully along the centre of the canal. Luke could see little beyond it but a green smudge. There was no way to get onto dry land and run. The distance to the bank was too great. Even if he'd been on top form, it was too far to jump. There was no escape to safety.

Somewhere close, an unemotional voice was giving instructions but Luke didn't catch the words.

There was only one thing to do. Using his long legs, Luke took off down the gangway that passed as a running track. At the end, instead of slowing to take the corner, he leapt up onto a crate and took off.

In his imagination, he flew. It must have been a split-second but it seemed that he hung in the air for a long time. Then he plunged down. He pitched into the canal as the boat exploded.

All around him, the water seemed to boil wildly. It was alive with surging air and fragments of wood. Buffeted, Luke rolled over and over, totally out of control. He grasped something big and solid but it was wrenched violently from his arms. He felt a stabbing in his side as if he'd been harpooned. There was air on his face and, the next moment, it had gone again. He was staring through rippling water at wreckage coming into and going out of focus.

And then there was silence. He was cast adrift like the rest of the flotsam.

A dented Malc hovered over the canal above the floating carnage of the explosion. He did not have the power to flip Luke's inert body over so that he could breathe. Gently, the mobile pushed him, still face-down, towards the water's edge.

Luke did not react to his feet touching land. Malc rotated his body until his hands made contact with the muddy bank. It was then that the forensic investigator stirred. Some instinctive desire for life kicked in. His fingers clenched, his elbows bent and he hauled half of his body up onto the earth. He rolled over, gagged and then breathed.

Malc was about to make for the nearest freeway when he heard a faint voice.

"Tell Jade. . ."

Luke's words faded away beyond human hearing. But, with his microphone adjusted to pick up the slightest sound, Malc recorded most of the message.

But that was all. Luke went limp and said no more.

Chapter Twenty-Eight

The two doctors stood in front of the light-wall and gazed at the emergency scan of Luke Harding's brain. The first examined the dark area above the left ear but Peter Sachs had seen enough. Unable to contain his emotions, he turned away.

The specialist said, "Well, we've caught it early. It's small, but. . ."

"It's inoperable," Dr Sachs mumbled.

"With conventional techniques, yes."

Peter stared at him. "What do you mean? Is there another way?"

"Things have moved on a bit in the past eleven years, Peter. I want to bring the Institute of Biomechanical Research in. Oscar Hislop's got an ultrasonic probe that heats cancer cells and kills them in seconds, leaving normal ones alone."

"I haven't heard of it."

"It's not exactly routine."

"You mean it's experimental. It hasn't been tried and tested."

The specialist nodded. "That's exactly what I mean. It's never been used on a human subject. It works on brain slices."

"Brain slices. That's a lot different from living brain

tissue inside a living boy. We're talking about my son!"

The first doctor studied the scan again and then said, "For this, it's all we've got."

On learning the discouraging diagnosis, The Authorities put out an immediate recall for Luke Harding's Mobile Aid to Law and Crime. "You will travel to your nearest forensic station for reprogramming and reassignment."

Malc transmitted an abrupt response. "Negative."

"What?" the voice of The Authorities snapped. "You will report to us for repair and to receive new duty programs."

Malc replied, "I am still under instruction from Forensic Investigator Luke Harding—"

"Impossible. His case has been concluded satisfactorily and he is unconscious."

"Confirmed. But he gave me a final instruction. I will complete the task."

"I'm overruling any such instructions. You will report—"

"I will report for reassignment once my final command is concluded," Malc insisted.

"Immediate recall. It seems your systems were more badly damaged in the explosion than your self-diagnosis estimated."

"I have logged your task for completion when I have spare resource." With that, the Mobile Aid to Law and Crime terminated the transmission.

If Malc had tried to order an electric cab to travel on his own, The Authorities' agents would have eavesdropped on his request and stopped him right away. Malc had to try a different tactic. Once he had explained his mission to Elisa Harding, she used her identity card to call him a cab.

Speeding towards Sheffield, Malc did not know The Authorities' procedure for dealing with a fugitive robot. His databases did not include any previous example of a renegade Mobile Aid to Law and Crime. It just did not happen. He assumed that agents would have already been assigned to the task of hunting him. To do so, they would probably be monitoring his location through his global positioning unit, but there was nothing he could do to stop that. Shutting down such a vital unit was impossible.

When the cab pulled up outside the ornate building of the Sheffield Music Collective, Malc did not hesitate. He requested access to interview Jade Vernon.

There was a delay of one minute and forty-one seconds before he got a response. Presumably Ms Vernon had agreed to meet him because the door slid back, allowing him to enter. Malc did not get as far as her mixing studio. She came out into the passageway and stared at the tattered mobile with her mouth open.

"Luke Harding has an inoperable brain tumour. He ordered—"

Jade shook her head and put up her hand. "What? You can't. . . I don't understand. There's some sort of mistake.

I'm working on a new song for him."

Malc was doing all that he could. He was incapable of tact. "The song may not be required. It may be curtains. He is seriously ill in York Hospital."

"But. . ."

At the end of the corridor, a team of agents clattered noisily through the door.

Realizing the urgency, Malc began, "Luke Harding ordered me to tell you. . ." But he didn't get any further.

The leader pointed some sort of metal probe at him and fired. At once, Malc lowered himself to the floor and his systems shut down.

"Sorry, Ms Vernon," she said. "This mobile's malfunctioning. It's been recalled for repair with immediate effect. Sorry to bother you."

"But he. . . it. . . was delivering a message."

"No chance," she said. As her team bundled the useless machine away, she explained, "Any communication wouldn't be valid. It might even have been garbled. The machine's programming got screwed up in an explosion. It was refusing to obey The Authorities. Unheard of. There'll be a big inquiry. It'll be dismantled bit-by-bit to see what went wrong."

Jade watched them retreat and swallowed her tears. She rushed back to her room to use the telescreen. On Friday, Luke had told her that his father's name was Peter Sachs and that he was a doctor at York Hospital. That was enough to get in contact and find out what was happening. That's what she needed most. News of Luke.

She should have been devastated that she had not heard his message, but she wasn't. It was enough that Malc had defied The Authorities in an attempt to tell her. Besides, she knew exactly what Luke would have said to her.

Luke found himself in a familiar place. He was lying down and above him was the stunning night sky, dotted with stars. There wasn't a murmur. No wind, no movement, no noise. Nothing. It was neither cold nor hot. He felt calm and peaceful, as if he'd abandoned all responsibility for himself. He was in someone else's hands now.

Then there was something. A sound. A melancholy series of chords, full of space. Sad but soothing. For a moment Luke thought that he was going to hear Jade's voice, but it wasn't that. It was internal. It was music in his head and his own diseased brain was conjuring the words. Beautiful words about stars. Worrying words about his life.

Before they die
They make the sweetest sound
Just for a moment
Then they're gone

When I die

She'll make the saddest sound
And then the world just carries on. . .

The lyrics ended abruptly but the music grew louder in his left ear, burning his brain with its intensity.

Chapter Twenty-Nine

In a private room, Peter Sachs looked at Jade across the motionless form of his son and said, "We wanted to meet you but. . . not like this. Sorry."

Jade was kneeling at Luke's bedside with both hands clutching his left arm. "You don't have to say sorry. It's not your fault."

Elisa was about to add something but swallowed her words. She looked pale and tormented.

"It's no one's fault," Jade said. "It's just. . . the way things are."

When Oscar Hislop walked into the room, all three of them gazed at him in anticipation. Their faces revealed different degrees of fear and impatience.

"Well?" Luke's father prompted.

Oscar didn't reply instantly so Jade leapt in. "Is he going to be all right?"

"Before I tell you what I think," Oscar said to Peter, "let me show you the before and after brain scans." Glancing occasionally at the telescreen, Oscar fiddled with the controller in his hands. "Ah. Here we go."

Two views of Luke's brain appeared side-by-side on the display. They were marbled grey with splashes of red and black. In perfect unison, the images zoomed to the area above his left ear and rotated.

Jade did not know what to look for. She didn't know good news from bad. Instead, she stared at Peter. With relief, she saw the anxiety in his face drop away as he examined the scans.

Peter turned towards Oscar and cried, "It's gone!"

Oscar nodded proudly. "The ultrasonic probe. I told Luke — it's the future for tricky tumours. I didn't know then that he'd be the first."

"Surgery couldn't have done anything like this," Peter muttered. "It's. . . fantastic."

Elisa stepped forward and gazed at the new brain scan as if it were an artistic masterpiece, as if she were in awe of it. "Is it all over, then?"

"No one can guarantee it won't come back — in time," Oscar answered. "But, if it did, it'd just need another treatment. That should be the end of it."

"But when he wakes up," Jade said, "will he be. . . you know. . . the same? He's got a hole in his brain, hasn't he? Will it affect him?"

"I don't know," Oscar admitted. "That's not my field. All I can tell you is he's got his life back. He's going to pull through."

Jade turned towards Dr Sachs.

"We've got to be grateful he's still with us, Jade. He might be exactly the same but yes, his brain's been damaged. He might be. . . a bit different."

"How do you mean?"

Peter shrugged helplessly. "We'll have to wait and see."

"But tell me he'll still be Luke. He'll still know me, won't he?"

Elisa put her hand on Jade's shoulder. "Why don't you put the headphones on him again and play him some more of your music? I'm sure he can hear it and it'll guide him back. He won't be so scared. He'll know he's not alone."

Peter nodded in agreement. "If he's listening to your music, he won't forget you."

The tune in Luke's head had changed. The sound reminded him of something bright yellow and round. He found it comforting. Eyes still closed, he murmured, "Turn it up, Malc."

Instead of an instant response to his instruction, there was a gasp like the sharp intake of human breath.

"Did you get that message to Jade?"

"No, he didn't. He tried, though," a voice answered. "You'll have to tell me yourself."

Luke's eyelids felt as if they'd been glued shut. He had to force them open. He was in a room. It took several seconds for a plain white ceiling to come into focus. "Where are the stars?" he asked. Then he levered himself up onto his elbows and looked around.

"Malc's not here," Jade said. "It's me." She clutched his bare arm and said, "See? Skin, not metal."

Luke gazed at the girl, puzzled. She seemed to be on the point of laughing or crying. He wasn't sure which. "Your hair's red."

She nodded. "That's how you like it best."

"Do I?"

"Yes."

"The colour of pomegranates and blood. And the noise a fire makes."

"Luke, I think you're a bit. . . Do you know who I am?"

He hesitated. He was about to admit that he didn't when his mind suddenly cleared. It was like a new dawn. The sun engulfed him with light and warmth. "Jade!"

"Good to have you back, FI Harding." She was smiling and sobbing at the same time now. "How's tricks?"

"I'm. . ." He thought about it for a moment, then he flung his arms around her. "I'm flying."